The E & N Escape

The Vancouver Island Mysteries Series, Volume 3
By P.N. Holland

Filidh Publishing

Copyright 2023 P.N. Holland (Revised Edition)
ISBN 978-1-927848-75-3
Filidh Publishing, Victoria, BC
Cover Design by Danny Weeds.
Cover Photography and Art credits: Shutterstock Photo ID: 620978588 credit: itman _47' Shutterstock Photo ID: 1151904692 credit: Pereslavtseva Katerina; Shutterstock Vector ID: 1842395944 credit: anttoniart; and Shutterstock Illustration ID: 2080318156 credit: Mia Stendal

First edition. March 5, 2020. Copyright © 2020 P.N. Holland.
Original Copyright © 2018 PN Holland

Also, by P.N. Holland
The Vancouver Island Mysteries Series:
>   The Saxe Point Park Mystery, Volume 1
>   The Lost Boys of Lampson, Volume 2
Vahldohr: Mellissadorha Series– Book One
>   Watch for more at https://pnholland.com/

****

To my Grandchildren; Ariel, Emily, Zachery, Brenan, Leyland, and all of my followers who keep me writing.

****

— CHAPTER ONE —

Purple Eyes

"Why are we going up island on an old train, Billy?" my sister, Sarah, asks.

"I already told you," I say, frowning at her while working my iPad. "We're writing an historical essay on the E&N Railroad."

"Yes," Ricky pipes in. "What better way to get a feel of the journey than a trip."

"But it smells musty and it's so slow. We'll never get to Nanaimo in time for my game," she says as she fingers her iPhone.

"Don't worry. There's lots of time to get you there. It's only ten o'clock in the morning and your game isn't until three."

"Yeah, we're even buying you lunch." Ricky wiggles his eyebrows.

"I know. It's just so boring."

"Well, read your book, or play on your iPhone or something." I say, rolling my eyes. At that point, she is so immersed in her phone that she doesn't answer. "I rest my case."

"Billy, we need to get some pictures from the Kinsol Trestle and at Cliffside, where The Last Spike was driven in by Sir John A. MacDonald, the first Prime Minister of Canada," Ricky reminds me.

"Don't worry. That's at the top of my list. You know, there's something I've not done yet."

"What's that?"

"Walk the trestle. What do you think?"

"That's swag, man," Ricky says. He is obviously game.

"You guys are crazy," my sister chimes in. "You're not allowed to do that, are you?"

"Actually, you are."

"Really?" Sarah shakes her head and goes back to her iPhone. Her fourteen years of experience not appreciating our adventure.

"Tell you what. You can film us." She just rolls her eyes at me.

"How much farther is it?" Ricky asks.

"Well..." I answer, pushing the keys of the iPad. "...let me see. Uh, here we go, about thirty minutes away."

"You're not really going to walk the trestle, are you?" my sister asks. "You'll never get them to stop the train." She shakes her head, blond curls bouncing with each movement.

"This train is a tourist attraction now. Not only do they stop there, but they give you pamphlets, sell souvenirs and take your picture as you walk it."

"What?" She looks shocked. "That's just crazy."

"No, sis, that's capitalism. Everything is worth something."

"It's the only way they can afford to keep the old E&N running," Ricky says. "They actually made a profit last year of two hundred and fifty thousand dollars or so. Of course, most of it was spent to upgrade the line and fix some of the old steam engines, but over fifty thousand tourists came to ride on it last year."

"Come and walk the trestle with us," I say.

"I don't think so." She giggles at something on her phone.

"Suit yourself, but there's a cool souvenir shop on the other side."

"The Kinsol trestle was built in the 1920's," Ricky says. "Here, let me look it up."

"Yeah, we'll need some of the historical details for our report. Mrs. Owens wants at least a ten-page document."

"Indeed, and with references. When is it due, again?"

"Two weeks from Friday, I think. Don't you have the assignment details there on your laptop?"

"Oh, yeah, just a sec. Friday, the seventeenth in History 12."

"Alright then, I also have a Political Science debate to write before then, how about you?"

"I've got to research for a Chemistry lab experiment on mixing organic compounds."

"Sounds like fun. Just don't create any Methamphetamines."

I laugh. "It's not that kind of lab, Ricky. Back to the task at hand, it says here that the Kinsol trestle was about 187 meters long and 38 meters high, one of the highest one's ever built."

"That's pretty cool. It would be fun to bungee jump off of, eh?"

"Yes, I guess if you're suicidal." Ricky snickers as I read further. "They started rebuilding it in 2010 and on July 28, 2011, it was reopened as part of the TransCanada Trail. The new tracks have only been on it for a few years. Before then it was like a glorified bike path. Now it's a tourist attraction almost as popular as Butchart Gardens in Victoria."

"When were the tracks put in?"

"In 2018, even the Prime Minister was there, sort of like the Sir John A. Macdonald ceremony. They put a spike in and everything."

"Really? Trudeau was there?" Ricky asks.

"Yeah, at the same place, Cliffside, and there's a second plaque there as well."

"Good thing cameras are on iPhones and iPads these days, eh?"

"Yup, sure makes it easy. We should be at Cliffside any minute." I look out the right-side window. "No signs."

"Don't worry," Ricky says, pulling a brochure out of his pocket. "It says here that the train stops there. We'll be able to get out and take pictures."

"That works for me."

About ten minutes later, we arrive at Cliffside. Sarah, totally absorbed in her iPhone, stays on board as Ricky and I hop out. I can hear the steam jettisoning out of the engine when we step down the metal stairway to the gravel beside the tracks. The cool, fresh air is a relief from the smoky smell of the train. A small group of tourists follows us up the path to the site of the Cliffside plaques. A small kiosk sits beside them filled with souvenirs; miniature plaques, flags, postcards, pictures, and of course various trinkets, candies and toys. I take several pictures of both plaques from every angle I

7

can manage while Ricky inspects the kiosk goodies. We buy some trinkets to use in our class presentation later. With the train stopped, I can hear the water from the river below swooshing over the rocks and fallen trees. The air is cool with a hint of winter coming, there's snow on the mountains above the tracks.

At the souvenir shop, an unusual girl, about our age, stands off to the side eyeing everyone. She has large, bright purple eyes and an iWatch-like disk strapped to her arm. Her clothes look as if they are form-fitted to her body, like spandex, kind of sexy. Even her shoes have no separation. Weird. She has gold wraparound dragon earrings that glow as if they have tiny batteries in them.

We make eye contact; she stares for several seconds as if reading my mind before diverting her gaze. I gesture to Ricky, who waves more pamphlets, and glances back at me. He casually steps toward the girl without eyeing her. She turns and bats her eyes at him as he walks past her. She raises her eyebrows and smiles at us. My hackles go up and I reach for my wand in my pocket and step forward.

"Hi," I say, smiling back. "I'm Billy, and this is my friend, Ricky."

"Hi, I'm Azandra. Happy to meet you," she replies, and reaches down to touch the iWatch thing on her arm. It's aimed at us so I suspect it takes our picture. Ricky quickly snaps a shot of her with his iPhone just as the engineer steps down from the train and shouts, "All aboard!" People start filing forward as we talk.

"You have very unusual eye color," I say. "Are they contacts?"

"Yeah, sort of, although a little more sophisticated," she answers.

"What do you mean?" Ricky asks.

"They're not just contacts. They're more like tiny computers."

"Really? What do they do actually?"

"It's complicated. I couldn't begin to explain it all. They're like cameras with special abilities. I think we better get onboard before the train leaves." She turns, grabbing the ladder and rushing up the stairs. We follow but lose her as she zips ahead and into another car.

"Billy, there you are." My sister tugs on my arm. I turn and snap at her, "What?" My gaze searches for the purple eyes.

"Well, you don't have to bite my head off," she says, crossing her arms and frowning. "How much longer is it to the trestle? I'm hungry, and you promised me lunch."

"Relax. We'll be there in a few minutes." I turn and head back to our seats. All we hear is the light murmur of people chatting and the click-clack of the wheels below us.

"I wonder where that girl is going?" Ricky asks, saying what I was thinking.

"I don't know, but I sure would like to talk to her again."

"Yeah, I can't get over those strange purple eyes. It felt like she was looking into my soul or something."

"Who are you guys talking about?" Sarah asks.

"Just a girl we met at the last stop," I answer.

"What was wrong with her eyes?"

"Nothing, it's just, they were purple in color and she said they had unusual abilities."

"What unusual abilities?" Her face scrunches up.

"We didn't have time to ask her because she jumped on the train too quickly," Ricky says.

"Sounds weird. What was she wearing?"

"That was strange too," I say. "Her clothes clung to her like they were spandex or something. Even her shoes were part of the one-piece outfit. Do you know any girls who wear clothes like that?"

"Not really," my sister answers. "My friend, Lolly, sometimes wears spandex, but usually when she's doing her workouts or track training. I've never seen a suit that included footwear before though."

"Maybe we can find her," Ricky says. "She's on the train somewhere."

"Well," I say, "there are only about six passenger cars. It shouldn't take that long. You and Ricky go towards the back and

9

I'll move to the front. Text me if you find her or if you don't, text me anyway when you reach the caboose."

Ricky and Sarah take off one way and I head in the other direction, carefully looking at all the seated people on both sides of the train. I get one ugly look from a girl with green hair and piercing blue eyes as I stare a little too long. I quickly apologize and hurry on to the last car before the engine. Nobody looks like the mysterious, purple-eyed beauty.

Just as I'm reaching for the door to the outside rail, Ricky texts me.

Ricky—No sign of her from this end.

Billy—Me neither. Come up to our seats. I'll meet you there.

When we meet up, Ricky says, "I don't see how she gave us the slip."

"The only place we didn't look is in the washrooms," Sarah says. "I'll check the women's; you check the men's." Just as we get back, together the train whistle blows and the E&N starts slowing down.

"Well, that was a bust. I don't see why she's not on the train," I say.

"Maybe she stepped off the train just before we got underway," Ricky reasons.

Sarah shrugs.

"We must be coming up to the Kinsol Trestle.

"You ready for the walk of destiny?" I tease.

"Yup. How about it Sarah? You game?"

"Like, no," Sarah says, "but don't be long because you still owe me lunch."

The sun is shining as we step off the train except for a mist rising around the trestle from the water below. Sarah sits on a bench under some trees beside a small café where several tourists are milling about looking at souvenirs, menus, and pamphlets. I take a look back as we reach the trestle. Nobody else is behind us. It feels a little strange as the fog surrounds us. A sudden chill wind creeps up and I zip my jacket up. I can't see in front, behind, or below as a shroud of greenish electricity sparks all around us.

"What the heck?" Ricky says, pulling his wand out as we both stop about halfway across. "Where did everything go?"

"And what's with all of that green static?"

— CHAPTER TWO —

Missing

Sarah rises from the bench where she's been texting her friend, looking for Ricky and Billy on the other side of the trestle, but all she can make out is half of the bridge covered in mist. *Where are those stupid boys?* She steps toward the overpass. *I guess I'll have to cross the river after all.* She walks slowly through the wet cloud until she reaches the halfway point, stops and peers at the other side, afraid to look down. She shivers with the cold as she scans the souvenir shop, the restaurant, people walking all around, but the boys are nowhere in sight. In panic mode, she runs the rest of the way across, searching every place she thinks they may have gone.

Frustrated, she takes out her cell, brings up her picture files until she finds some of the boys.

"Have you seen these boys?" she asks the souvenir vendor. He studies the pictures carefully. "No, sorry. Were they on the train?"

"Yes, thanks anyway." Sarah rushes around asking several people, but nobody has noticed them. It's as if they've disappeared. She sits on a bench and looks back towards the train. Maybe I missed them when they crossed back. I spend too much time on this stupid phone. She stuffs it into her pocket, dashes back over the trestle, and searches the other side. Not a sign of them and not one single person has seen them. Her last option is to check the train. She scours every car and both washrooms, even when a gentleman yells at her as she enters the men's washroom. She ignores him, pushing in the stalls anyway before slipping out again. *What do I do now?*

She's startled when the train's whistle blows and the engineer hollers, "All aboard!" *Should I stay on the train or get off and hope they show up? All of their stuff is still on the train. I'd better stay aboard. Besides, if they show up, they'll find their way to Nanaimo and expect me to be there.* She goes back to their seats and sits down. *I hope they're okay.* She texts her friend Lolly, who has already arrived in Nanaimo with her mom.

Lolly—Don't worry, they're big boys, they'll catch up with us later. They probably got distracted by some girl. LOL

Sarah—Okay, I'll see you soon. You're still meeting me at the train station, right?

Lolly—Yup, have you had lunch?

Sarah—No, the stupid boys were supposed to spring for it.

Lolly—Right. Well not to worry, my mom will buy it for us.

Sarah—Great. Thank you. See you soon.

Putting her phone back in her pocket, Sarah reaches up into the shelf above, making sure the boys' backpacks are still there. Thank goodness, they are, along with Billy's laptop. *If he'd lost that Mom would kill him.* Her stomach growls as she curses the boys for her missed lunch. She sinks back in her seat, pulls out her iPhone and plays 'Alysha's Witches', her favorite magic game. She started playing a week ago and is already on level 12.

Less than an hour later she is struggling to carry all of their backpacks off the train at Nanaimo Station. People, cars, and buses are all around. She looks, but can't see Lolly and her mom anywhere. They'd better be here. Her panic causes her to trip on the stairs down from the platform and she cries out as she falls. A lady in front of her turns, reaches up and catches her, stopping her fall.

"Oh, thank you," Sarah says as she straightens up, eyeing the woman who let's go of her and steps back.

"You're welcome. Are you okay?"

"Yes," Sarah mumbles, trying to see the woman's face but the sun is in her eyes.

"That's a lot of luggage for one person. Can I help you?" Sarah is surprised when she notices the lady's dragon necklace sparkling over her bosom and glimpses the woman's face. Purple eyes? Yup, she has dragon earrings as well. But Billy had said that the girl he saw was young. This lady is at least 20, more likely 30.

"Thank you," Sarah says as the lady picks up a backpack.

"Is someone meeting you?" dragon lady asks.

"Yes, my friend and her mom, but I don't see them yet."

"I can wait with you if you like. Could you use something to drink? Coffee or tea?"

"Oh, I would love a Pepsi, if you don't mind."

"Let's go over to the café. I can see a vacant table outside. It will be nice to sit in the sunshine on such a beautiful day." She turns, her necklace glinting back and forth as she hoists the heavy backpack over her shoulder with no problem at all. Sarah follows, noticing the tight-fitting clothing hugging the woman's ample backside and the shoes like booties seemingly part of the outfit. Weird, but practical.

"I couldn't help but notice all of your luggage. Are you moving or something?" dragon lady asks as they sip their drinks.

"No, some of it is my brother's and his friend's stuff. I'm meeting them in Nanaimo," Sarah answers, a little reluctant to divulge the extent of her dilemma.

"Oh," purple eyes says. "By the way, I'm Lenora."

"I'm Sarah. Pleased to meet you."

"Do you live here?"

"No, I'm just coming to play a soccer game."

"Do you play for a school team?"

"No, it's a community team, the Gordon Head Griffins. We play against various city teams on the island. Are you travelling up island to meet someone?"

"Sort of. I'm on a business trip."

"What's your business?"

"I'm a travel agent."

"Oh, so you arrange trip details for people on holidays and business?"

"Something like that, yes; mostly foreign clients."

"From other countries, like France and England?"

"Like that, yes, sort of."

As they continue talking, Lolly and her mom walk up behind dragon lady. "You okay, Sarah?" Lolly asks as purple eyes turns to view them.

"Who's your friend?" Lolly's mom asks.

"Hi, I'm Lenora."

"Hello, I'm Kassandra, Lolly's mom. Thanks for helping Sarah."

"Of course. Well, I really should be going before I miss my appointment." She rises and glances back at Sarah. "Nice to meet you, Sarah. Good luck in your game." Lenora blinks twice at them, turns, and heads towards the café parking lot.

"Thank you," Sarah says as Lolly and Kassandra sit down.

"She looks a little different," Kassandra says.

"Yes, did you see her clothes and those eyes? I've never seen purple contacts before," Lolly says.

"I don't think they're contacts," Sarah says.

"Really? I've never seen anyone born with purple eyes," Kassandra says. "Anyway, what happened to the boys?"

"That's the strange part. They were walking across the Kinsol Trestle when they disappeared."

"Disappeared?" Lolly's mom raises her eyebrows. "Maybe they just got caught up talking to somebody."

"Like a girl?" Lolly teases.

"But, I looked for them everywhere and talked to everybody. Nobody had seen them after the trestle."

"I wouldn't worry," Lolly's mom says. "I'm sure we'll see them in Nanaimo at the field. In the meantime, let's get some lunch."

Sarah raises her eyebrows and presses her lips together.

"It'll be okay," her friend says, giving her a hug. Sarah sighs, grabs her luggage and heads for the car.

— CHAPTER THREE —

Somewhere Else

Oh, my aching head. It's freezing! What the hey? Where am I? Antarctica? I'm in the middle of a white, winter wonderland. Had I known I would have worn my mukluks. "Hold on, we were on the train, crossing the trestle. I don't see the train, rails, or the trestle. Billy-boy, you're not in Kansas anymore," I say to nobody save for a lone wolf howling in the distance. "Brrrr, mouth full of snowflakes." *Hmm, a long ridge of high trees ahead. I need to get out of this wind and cold, and find shelter before I freeze.* "Ricky! Ricky!" I yell. No sign of him. *This is like slogging through three feet of sand.* "Ricky! Ricky!" I call again, listening as my words disappear into the woods. No response. *I hope he's okay. And what about Sarah?*

Several steps along the tree line I find a path with what looks like footprints going into the forest. "Ricky! Ricky!" I holler again and listen. Nothing. I trudge along the path trying to stay in the footprints already there, to keep my runners from disappearing in the white depth. At least the trees supply some shelter from the snow and wind. Deeper in the forest, the dark is quickly surrounding me; nightfall is not far away. I need shelter, fire, and water. Searching for a protected open space among the trees, I trudge on, distracted by the strange animal sounds: deep howls and a weird screeching like some demented bird.

After several minutes, I break through the brush into a sheltered spot, perfect for camping. Looking around, there's no sign of animals. Plenty of broken, dry branches on the trees for firewood and shelter allow me to tear off fir branches, pick up fallen twigs on the ground, and strip off the thicker ones for poles to make a lean-to. Next, a fire; piling up small twigs and birch bark I lean over them.

"*Ignis*," I say, tapping my wand on the twigs. Flames leap up catching the kindling and bark. Good thing magic works here or

I would be in big trouble. Now, I need water. Let's see, take some snow and liquefy it, that's the plan. I know there's a spell for that if I can think of it. Water is '*Aqua*' and thaw is '*Regelo*'. I pick up and roll the snow into a ball in my hands. "*Aqua regelo*." After four handfuls of cool water, I feel much better except for my freezing fingers, but they are soon thawed out from the heat of the flames.

Okay, now for some food, but before I can entice a rabbit to come to me, a glistening bluish object flies through the woods towards me. It stops about thirty feet from my camp, a shiny, circular metallic object hovering silently. My wand shakes when I aim it, ready for a fight as it slips forward making no sound. About twenty feet away it stops, a shiny hatch lowers from it and a person descends the ramp.

"Who are you?" I yell, but she ignores my cry, touches her hand to her right wrist, and sends a bright greenish light towards me. I cover my eyes expecting the brightness to hurt, but it doesn't. It just warms me.

A voice starts speaking in my head. "Do not fear. I am Azandra. We met at the train. Remember?"

"Yes," I say in my head, my wand still ready. "Where am I, and where is Ricky?"

"You are in the future and your friend is safe. Somehow you were separated in the transfer."

"Transfer? Really? What year is it?"

"Just wait and I will bring the orb to you and get you out of the cold, then I can explain everything. Okay?"

"Alright."

I lower my wand and watch as she goes back in. The beam stops, the hatch closes, and the orb zips right up in front of me. Heat emanates from it as it glows like a big Christmas ornament. The hatch opens again and Azandra steps out and reaches her hand towards me. The inside looks warm and welcoming. With mixed feelings of worry and relief I accept her offer and step into the orb. The hatch closes and we rise swiftly above the trees. Funny, there is no sensation of motion as I watch the land and snow below whiz by, right through the floor. Great view.

"Billy, I'm sorry that you got misplaced, but you are safe now."

"Okay, but tell me what year it is and what is going on."

"It is the tenth year of the new age, or if you'd rather, in the old calendar, about 2066."

"2066? What do you mean by 'the new age'?"

"Well after World War III, the destruction caused an environmental collapse and a polar shift that changed the world's climate enough to cause a new ice age."

"What? World War III? Ice age?"

"Yes, after the religious crisis in the Middle East, in 2025, the Iranians and the Russians overran Iraq, attacked Israel and half of Europe. The USA, Canada, France and Britain entered the war against Russia, Syria, Afghanistan and Iran. North Korea sent nuclear missiles over China causing a million casualties and..."

"Whoa, I get it. How did a polar shift happen?"

"In 2029, a nuclear bomb set off a super volcano in southern Asia sending enough ash into the atmosphere to block the sun for several years, which caused the worldwide temperature to lower by more than twenty-five degrees. Then a huge 10.0 mega earthquake occurred in California in 2031, sinking the west coast, flooding the center of North America, causing tsunamis half a mile high to wash over the Pacific and smash Japan, Indonesia, China, New Zealand and Australia. Another massive volcano erupted in Alaska, which moved the earth's axis more than 12 degrees, shifting the poles, sinking Japan, half of China and eastern Russia, while uncovering Antarctica. All of North America is covered with ice now. More than six billion people are dead since the catastrophe.

"Oh, my God!" The shock of her words hits me like a sledgehammer, and I feel dizzy, my heart pounding.

"Are you okay?" she asks as I hold onto the wall.

"Why am I here?"

"We need you and Ricky to help us."

"How can we help? This is the future, right? What can we do?"

"You are a wizard and have the ability to go back and forward in time. We need you to help us identify and stop a wizard who started this disaster, before he causes more havoc."

"Seriously? A wizard did this? Change the future? That's not possible, is it?"

"No, it is not, he just set things in motion, but you and Ricky can help fight him now."

"Why don't you and your people just use your technology against him?"

"We have tried, but it is no match for his magic. Your ability is extremely rare. As it is, we had to reach into the past to find you. We have not been able to find anyone in our time with your abilities, as yet." I noticed tall buildings below us housed in a huge dome. A city glittered below our feet. Capsules like the one we were in, zipped all over the skies inside the dome. I could also make out trees, fields with crops, rivers, lakes and even small mountains.

"Wow," I say. "What is this place?"

"New Albion, one of the few cities rebuilt after the shift."

"What is the Earth's population now?"

"About half a billion we are aware of."

"What do you mean?"

"There are some who choose to not live with us in the protected cities. The Outlanders' numbers are harder to determine. Our scientists estimate around half a million or so, not including the off-planet that is."

"Off-planet?"

"Yes, we have five small colonies on the moon which were set up prior to the catastrophe, around 2027. They are working on several more domed cities as we speak."

"Wow, the world has really changed. Anything else I should be aware of ?"

"Yes, we have other allies. You may not be aware but there are several groups of aliens who have been monitoring and interfering in our affairs for thousands of years. Some of them are trying to help our race while others are trying to eliminate or control us."

"My God, this is getting complicated, but I've been aware of ET's since I was a child, so I'm not surprised. How do we enter this domed city?"

"There are several hatches which can be opened by the inhabitants. They scan all ships before that happens. It only takes a few minutes, and we will be inside."

I wait patiently while we remain stationary for a few moments. A yellow tractor beam catches us, and we move through an open, clear hatch in the dome. Once inside, the beam stops, the hatch closes and we zip to a landing pad on the top of a very high building. I can see several important looking people standing, waiting for us to disembark the orb. Stepping out, I hesitantly breathe in the air that seems fresh and odorless.

"Don't worry, the atmosphere is clean and breathable, no nuclear poisons, balanced gases, and plenty of oxygen." Exhaling and trying to keep calm, feeling like I'm on another planet, I watch as the welcoming group comes closer. Two beings who must be aliens because their features are very different catch my eyes. One looks like a giant insect, a praying mantis; the other a tall, grey entity with big oval eyes, an oversized head and thin body. Each of its hands has three long fingers. I breathe deep and face them.

"Welcome to New Albion," a tall human lady with flowing red hair, purple eyes, and a blue cape over the tight spandex-like covering, says as she extends her gloved hand. "I am the Council President, Rhunella." The top of her outfit has a logo on it that looks like a picture of our solar system.

"Thank you." I say, shaking her hand. "Where's Ricky?"
"Ah, yes, he's fine, just busy talking to the Galactic Council."

"What is that?"

"A group of alien and human leaders; there will be plenty of time to explain it all to you, but first you must be tired and hungry. Come, eat and rest."

"Follow me," Azandra says. Nervously, I walk past the welcoming party shaking hands and trying to avoid their searching gazes. Inside, we pass stairs to an elevator that carries us sideways, then down a few levels before it stops. We step out into an open space with several people scurrying about much like an office. They carry clear tablets with information on them, and on a far wall, there's a giant monitor with about ten different images on it, of people and places. "This is our Central Control Agency or CCA for short. The government is able to monitor all areas of our city to determine activities of interest and trouble spots. It's a bit invasive on our privacy, but such is the price for security these days."

"Doesn't seem a lot different from what was happening in my time, with computer monitoring, iPhone spy software, the cloud. It seems Big Brother is always watching."

"Unfortunately, not everybody can be trusted, even in your future, as you can imagine."

"I was hoping we would be past this by now, but I guess it's the price we pay for being human. Do aliens have the same trust issues?"

"Some do, some not so much, like the Alleurians, who are telepathic, so it is hard to hide harmful or deceptive thoughts."

"Where are they from?"

"Originally? Saggitarious, but they have been in our solar system for several centuries. They travel using wormholes, which drastically reduces the time of space travel. We are just learning how to use them ourselves."

"Wow. You mean we could travel to other planetary systems?"

"Yes, other dimensions as well."

She stops and opens a door along the corridor we've been walking through. A large apartment stands before me with windows showing a bustling city below, all the amenities of a house including a full bathroom and kitchen. "Get yourself washed and fed. There are clean clothes in the bedroom closet and food and drink in the kitchen. I will call you with the Intertab in a few hours."

"The Intertab? What's that?"

"A flat, clear tablet on the living room table. It will be the one talking or singing to you."

"Okay," I say, scratching my head.

"Don't worry," she says as she puts her hand on my shoulder, "You'll get acclimatized fairly quickly."

— CHAPTER FOUR —

Game Time

Sarah jumps to the left avoiding number 13, a big girl playing defense for the Nanaimo Spirit, and kicks a pass to Lolly, who tips it up and over the goalie. She cheers and dashes over to congratulate her friend as several teammates join them in a group hug. They're winning 3-2 and there is only five minutes left in the second half.

As they move back to the center of the field she notices Lolly's mom screaming from the stands, but she's not surprised by the cheering. It's the lady standing, clapping beside her that catches her eye. It's that lady with the purple eyes. Why is she at my soccer game? Distracted, Sarah misses her check and chases after her, but the ball is passed and a shot on goal ties the game.

"How did she get by you?" Lolly asks.

"I wasn't paying attention. Sorry."

"Well, let's get it back. We still have time."

On the faceoff, Lolly passes the ball to Cynthia, the midfielder, who dishes it ahead to Sandra, the right winger. Meanwhile, Sarah is racing down the middle to the 8-yard box. She circles and raises her hand as she avoids her check. Sandra spots her, nods, and Sarah sprints for the goal as Sandra sends it forward in the air. The ball is knocked down by a defender, but Sarah steals it as it bounces off the girl's chest and boots it past the keeper.

"Yes!" Sarah yells, and her teammates rush forward piling on top of her. When she gets back to the center of the field, she looks at the ref. "How much time?"

"Two minutes," he says after looking at his watch.

Then he blows his whistle, and the Spirit forward passes the ball back to the center midfielder. The girl captures it and boots it forward to their left winger who easily brings it to ground and passes to the left forward. Lolly is on her and bumps her off the ball, takes it back and passes it to Sarah who is tackled by a Spirit midfielder who kicks the ball forward to the right winger. She charges up the field and curls right to protect the ball, then makes an incredible air pass to the right forward who heads the ball toward

23

the net. Luckily, Heather, the Griffin's keeper, is equal to the task and taps the ball over the net. The ref blows his whistle, and the two teams prepare for a Spirit corner from the right side. Sarah nervously marks the right winger as the ball is kicked and curls sharply to the goal front. A tall Spirit midfielder jumps to head the ball, but Heather jumps too and grabs the ball as the tall girl knocks her to the ground. The Griffin's keeper shouts in pain while falling to the ground, but hugs the ball. The ref, glancing at his watch, blows his whistle three times announcing that the game is over. The Griffin supporters in the crowd shout and clap their hands as the teams congratulate each other and line up to shake hands.

After the game, Sarah, Lolly, Kassandra and Lenora go out to dinner.

"How did you know where the game was?" Sarah asks Lenora. "And why did you come watch it anyway?"

"Kassandra told me it was at Legion Field. That was easy to find on GPS." Lolly's mom frowns and shakes her head. "You mentioned it, but that doesn't matter. I came because I wanted to see how you would do and I felt sorry for you when you told me about your brother and his friend. Have they shown up yet?"

"No," Sarah says. "I don't understand where they've gone."

"Yes," Kassandra says. "It's strange. They've always been pretty responsible."

"Should we contact the police or something?" Lolly says.

"Let's finish our dinner, then we'll go to the po- lice station," Kassandra says.

"I'd better call my mom," Sarah says and picks up her iPhone. The other end rings and rings without any answer. "Come on, mom, pick up." The call goes to voice mail. "Mom, it's me. I'm still in Nanaimo with Lolly and her mom. Billy and Ricky have been missing since this morning. We're going to the police station to report their disappearance. Please call back as soon as you can."

"I'm sure there is a reasonable explanation for where they are, Sarah." Kassandra says, reaching over and hugging Sarah. "Don't worry, they'll show up."

"I—I guess so. This isn't the first time they've gone missing. Last summer Billy was away for three days before we found out he was exploring a cave with Ricky in Sooke. Mom was pretty upset with him because he hadn't contacted her. He said there was no cell reception."

"Yes, young men tend to be less concerned about who might be worrying about them than what they're into at the time," Lenora says.

Sarah pushes her plate away, grabs her jacket and phone then gets up. "Well, I can't eat anymore. Let's go to the police station now."

--*-*-*

"Well, that was a waste of time," Sarah says, a big frown on her face. "How come we have to wait twenty-four hours for them to be really missing? It's like they don't believe us or something."

"Standard procedure," Lolly's mom says.

"Yeah, that's pretty stupid," Lolly says, looking as upset as Sarah.

"I've got some serious contacts," Lenora says. "I'll let you know if I find out anything. Sarah, what's your cell number?" She pulls out a small tablet.

Sarah gives her the phone number.

"Got it, I'll talk to you later," Lenora says as she opens her blue rental car.

After Lenora leaves, Kassandra says, "Sarah, we'd better get back to the hotel."

On the way to the hotel, Sarah's mom calls and Sarah explains what's happened. "Mom says if we haven't heard from them in the next twenty-four hours to call her back and she'll drive up," Sarah says. "Okay." Kassandra pulls into the hotel parking lot.

Later, while sleeping, Sarah has a weird dream about her brother and Ricky fighting some strange dude with a red robe, flashing a wand and it looks like they're in a cloud or mist or someplace like a marsh. It's really cold with snow piled up, and a rocky overhang with a cave and light twinkling out of the entrance. She sees strange creatures too, sort of human, but with big heads and three fingered hands, red eyes, wearing metallic suits. They're floating in the dark, snowy air. "Ricky! Look out!" she screams, and wakes up in a cold sweat.

"Are you okay?" Lolly asks from beside her. Sarah sits up.

"I'm sorry, but I saw Billy and Ricky and they were being attacked by these strange creatures and—"

"You just had a bad dream, that's all," Lolly says. A moment later, her mom comes from the other room with a robe on.

"Are you guys okay? I heard a scream."

"Yes, mom, Sarah just had a bad dream."

"You okay?" Kassandra asks moving closer.

"Yes, it just seemed so real." Sarah rubs her eyes.

"Do you want some tea or something, dear? I've got chamomile."

"Yes, that would be nice."

"You too?" Kassandra asks her daughter.

"Yes, please."

The two girls get up from the bed and sit on the couch. Lolly's mom sets the kettle on to boil in the adjacent kitchen.

"Now, tell me about this dream," Lolly says.

Sarah tells both of them about the strange dream.

"I think you're just worried about your brother, dear," Kassandra says as they're sipping tea.

"I guess so."

"Best to just wait and see if they show up tomorrow. They know our hotel, don't they?" Kassandra asks.

"Yes, mom made sure we were both aware of everything for this trip. They've probably got themselves into something interesting as usual. They're always doing stupid things like this."

"Yeah, boys, what do we expect?" Lolly says, "They're all so irresponsible."

"They're not human until they're at least thirty." Lolly's mom laughs. "Take your father for example, he still does stupid things."

"Like when he got drunk at the last Christmas party and fell into the pool? That was pretty funny," Lolly says. Sarah offers a half-smile, her thoughts remaining on the boys and that dream. She'd had dreams before which turned out to be partly true. Her mom told her that she has the same gift, although sometimes it seems to be more of a curse, like when her gramma died in a terrible fire. Not all ESP is desirable, that's for sure.

The next day, Sarah's mom calls and explains that she was at a conference, and she'd left her cell at home. Sarah tells her what she knows, and her mom says that she will come up if they don't show up today. So, Sarah, Lolly and her mom do what all red-blooded ladies like to do, they go shopping in Nanaimo. Around lunchtime, while eating in a small restaurant, Lenora appears as if out of nowhere and sits down with them.

"Hello, ladies," she says, sliding into the empty chair at their table by the window.

"Hi," Kassandra and the girls say back.

"How did you find us?" Lolly asks.

"There are not that many malls in this city, so it was relatively easy."

"So, did you find out anything?" Sarah asks.

"No," Lenora says, "but I have some key people looking for them. They are the best there is in finding missing persons."

— CHAPTER FIVE —

Galactic Council

"William! William! It's time to awaken."

"What the...Is that you, Mom?" I roll over on the bed and look wearily at the doorway. Nobody there.

"William!"

"That's not my mother and I'm not home." I remember. "I'm in the future with Azandra, and Ricky. Where is he?" I mumble as a voice sings to me from the other room.

"Time to wake up, William. You need to get ready for the council."

"Alright, already, I'm up," I shout to the voice and throw the sheets back, noticing that clothes are arranged neatly on the settee beside me. Everything is clean, almost too clean; more like sterilized. *Makes sense, after all, I am sort of an alien from another time and could be carrying bacteria from the past. These future humans and aliens may be susceptible to viruses and germs, who knows?* Dressed, a strangely clothed alien looks back at me; high cropped collar, tight jacket, synthetic, all one outfit including soft shoes; very comfortable actually. All I need is a brush to keep my hair down. Stumbling to the bathroom I find some lubricant to relax my curls and brush them down. My forelock tumbles into my eyes. I blow it out of my face, but it doesn't help. *Oh, well, there are some things that won't be tamed.*

A knock at the door gets my attention. Stepping into the hall, I open the door by touching it and it slides to the left, disappearing. Azandra stands before me.

"Good, you are ready," she says, smiling.

"Ready for what?"

"To meet the council and see Ricky. Remember? Did you eat and rest?"

"Yes, I remember. Just a little tired I guess."

"Well, it's not every day that you travel forty years in time."

"Thank goodness. How much time would have passed back in my time?"

"Our current scientists and the aliens tell us that it is fluid so it depends on space and speed. Your time is probably only a few days later, but since I visited you in your time it has been about two weeks here."

"Using magic has the same effect so it's hard to change time's fluidity."

"Exactly. We'd better make our way to the meeting now."

"Oh, okay." I say, following her down the corridor. My apartment door closes of its own accord and locks. A mental note enters my mind, to ask her how the doors work for re-entry. In the elevator, we go down, then right and down some more. The door opens, where several people and aliens mill about at the front of this huge room, while others are seated in several rows facing the front. It's bright but there are no noticeable lights—it's as if the walls are made of light, very effective, but not hard on the eyes. The soft floor we walk on actually relaxes my feet.

"Go right up to the front," Azandra says as I pass the front row of chairs. Ricky is sitting on the other side of the front table.

"Billy, you made it," he says as I stop in front of him.

"You okay?" I ask.

"Yup, I'm alright. What happened to you?"

"Apparently, I got lost in the transfer, but Azandra found me and brought me here. Weird future, eh?"

"You got that right, but then again, I'm not too surprised considering what was happening in our time."

"Billy, we need to sit down on the other side," Azandra says, taking my hand and leading me to a seat beside Ricky. Then she sits beside me. Her perfume or something like it smells good. The whole room is looking at me.

Rhunella, wearing a green outfit this time, stands and raises her hands. Everyone stops talking. "Welcome, all delegates from outlying systems and the planets of our solar system. It is our great honor to be with you today. Also, as you have heard, we have the two earth magicians, Billy Maclean and Ricky Stevens present." She pauses while several delegates clap. "They are here to assist us in tracking down the disruptive wizard of the Outlands, Seth Mohryia, or whatever he calls himself now." As she pauses again, a rather tall man wearing a dark outfit, his reddish eyes shining, stands. "You have a question or comment, Rodan, Leader of the Lunar States?"

"Yes. I would like to know what abilities these young humans have that make them so important to our cause."

"Fair enough, Honored Regent. Perhaps Azandra, their advocate could enlighten us," the president says, waving her arm in our direction.

"Of course, Honored Regent," Azandra says, rising beside me. "The only way to fight Mohryia is by using his own methods, and these two mere humans are also wizards, able to travel through time and cast spells against evil."

Many of the audience clap, but the regent from the moon folds his arms and eyes us suspiciously.

"Perhaps a small demonstration is in order," he says. "Could they show us some of these skills now?"

"I don't think that is necessary," Rhunella says. "There will be plenty of time for them to use their abilities. Right now, they need to be brought up to speed in order to have success over this villain." Several delegates voice their dissent with "no's" and "boo's".

"We have been told falsehoods before, Madam President," Rodan says. Many voices agree with him.

The lack of belief in our abilities bothers me, and I look at Ricky and Azandra trying to decide what to do. Azandra is about to speak, but I rise and the crowd stops chattering to hear me. "I'm sure we can show you a sample of our magic. Ricky..." I pause and signal him with my hands, and he rises too. "...are you ready to show our quests?" Ricky nods.

"*Fac mihi interitum,*" I say, tapping my wand on my head and the crowd goes silent as I disappear in front of their eyes.

"*Fac mihi interitum,*" Ricky says, mimicking me with the same result.

"*Ubi es, Ricky?*" I say and he becomes visible to me. He has moved in front of the president.

"*Ut mihi apparet,*" I say, and appear right in front of Rhunella, who starts for a second, then laughs.

"*Ut mihi apparet,*" Ricky says and appears beside Rodan. He starts briefly, then smiles.

The crowd claps and Rodan raises his hand.

"Yes, Regent?" Rhunella says.

"Thank you, young wizards, for dispelling the rumors that you are not who you appear to be. I look forward to your help in finding and dealing with Mohryia."

"You're welcome," Ricky and I say at the same time, lowering our wands in salute.

"Thank you, Rodan," the president says and then she acknowledges another delegate; this one is a tall grey whose big, dark eyes seem to bore right through me. "Yes? Arnon, Representative of the Martian Outpost of the Alien Alliance."

"Thank you, Billy and Ricky, and welcome." Ricky and I nod back. "I understand you have had other experiences with wizards?"

"Yes," I answer, "with a disembodied spirit who used magic against us."

"And how did you subdue him?"

"Every entity has a spiritual connection they use in their magic. Finding and using that connection against them usually gives us the knowledge to disarm and eventually subdue them."

"Yes, I would agree that the energy or, as you call it, spiritual connections do show us the way to interfere with negative entities. You would simply call them evil?"

"Yes, I suppose it's the same thing," I say.

"Thank you." He sits down.

"Are there any more questions for our two gifted humans?" Rhunella asks. Nobody raises their hand. "Well then, we'll dismiss this meeting for now and confer with the wizards on a strategy to defeat Mohryia. Thank you all for attending."

The audience claps and slowly departs the room. Rhunella invites us to sit down around the main table where Azandra, Rodan, Arnon and six other entities are now seated.

"Azandra," Rhunella says, "can you tell us the latest information on Mohryia?"

"Yes, he was last seen outside New Albion, just a few days ago. We think he may have been aware of the arrival of Billy and Ricky. He didn't enter the city for fear of being caught by our sensors. Even with his great ability he still cannot hide from our technology. Instead, it is suggested that he has spies among our ranks." Azandra pauses and the entities around the table look at each other with suspicion. "So, we must be vigilant at all times and in all circumstances."

"We have technology filters which should help detect any spying or deceptive behaviors," Rhunella says.

"Yes, but we also must be careful to guard Billy and Ricky as well," Rodan says. "Remember what happened to our last searchers?" Ricky and I look at each other, eyebrows raised.

"Indeed," Rhunella says. "That is why we have operatives in all times and at all places of investigation. The wizards will not be alone to face Mohryia."

"What about Sarah?" I ask. "My sister must be worried sick by now and she has a psychic ability which can link to us."

"We will try to keep her out of this for now, but if necessary we may have to involve her, especially if Mohryia uses her as a bargaining chip," Rhunella says. "Azandra, you should set up the transfer back to their time right away. This will help our efforts and keep Billy's sister and others in the dark as to their real mission."

"Right away. Boys, let's go." Ricky and I jump up.

"Be careful," Rhunella says to us, and the rest of the inner council nod their heads.

CHAPTER SIX

The Search

In the elevator, we travel up and sideways. When it stops, the door opens to a room with a clear globe in the center, big enough to contain a few people, surrounded by machines that look like generators of strange green energy waves, which are turned down as we enter.

"Are we ready?" Azandra asks a man in a white suit standing in front of a panel with a series of dials and different colored lights.

"Yes, Councilor, all is ready," he says.

"Good. Boys, your clothes are fresh and ready for you to change into again. You'll find them in the room to your right." She points.

"Right." Ricky follows me into the room. Our clothes are neatly piled on top of a table with chairs beside it. Everything is there including our shoes. We quickly change.

"Are you ready to travel again?" I ask Ricky. "Do we have a choice?"

"No, I guess not."

"What if all of this is a sham and these people are actually the perpetrators of this future?" he asks.

"Do you really think so?"

"I don't know. I just wonder about it all. You have to admit it's a pretty fantastic story they've told us."

"I guess we'll find out, Ricky."

"Yup, here we go, buddy," he says, and we leave the room. As soon as we enter the departure site, I can hear the machinery start to churn up the green energy, attacking my ears with high frequency waves. My hair stands on end and a sensation of suction hits my body.

"Enter the pod," the man in white says. Azandra goes ahead of us into the globe. There are four seats in it which we immediately occupy. "Strap yourselves in," he continues. We follow Azandra's lead and do so. "You will depart as soon as the wave variance reaches the proper frequency."

As the sound rises, the green energy surrounds the bell and we find ourselves looking through a haze and the room waivers as if we are underwater. After several seconds, an intense white light floods the pod and we can no longer see the room around us. The green ripples flash louder until suddenly, everything disappears and we're flying through the ether. Time and space are gone. The intense pressure on my body makes it difficult to breathe as I await our arrival to who knows where.

In minutes, we arrive in the middle of an empty green meadow. We're still in the pod. Azandra pushes a sequence of buttons and the globe surrounding us disappears.

"Where did the pod go?" I ask.

"I've sent it back to my time," she answers.

"How are we going to travel back to your time then?" Ricky asks.

"It's okay, I know where the natural portals are and I have the sequencer to send us there," she says. "Now, when we meet up with your sister and friends you must tell them that you were busy doing research on your project."

"Don't worry," I say, "I've got that covered."

"Let's go then." Azandra leads us out of the meadow onto a paved road. Twenty minutes later we stop in front of the hotel where Sarah should be staying. We find her room number from the front desk and proceed to her floor.

"Where were you guys?" Sarah asks when she greets us at the door. "I was just about to call mom because you've been gone for hours."

"Yeah, sorry about that," I say, grimacing and trying to look apologetic. "We got caught up in our research on the E&N Railway. We met an elderly gentleman who used to be a conductor on the route between Nanaimo and Victoria and he told us all about the old days, locomotives, accidents, broken bridges and even a near catastrophe. How did your game go?"

"Good, we won by one goal so it was a close game. Lolly and her mom should be back shortly. Who's your friend?"

"This is Azandra, the girl we met on the train. Her grandfather is the old conductor I was telling you about."

"Pleased to meet you," Azandra says stepping forward.

"Likewise," Sarah says. "You have beautiful eyes."

"Thank you. So, do you."

"You're the second person to have purple eyes. Do you know a lady called Lenora?"

"No," Azandra says. "Boys, I have to leave now. I'll see you later."

"Right, okay," I say. Ricky nods his head and she leaves. "Would you call mom and tell her we're okay?"

"Sure." Sarah pulls out her iPhone and calls. "Hi, mom, yes they're back. They were doing research on their Socials project." She stops and listens. "Yes, we're fine, don't worry. We'll see you tomorrow at the train station."

Later at the Nanaimo depot, Billy spies Azandra walking toward them. "It's nice of you to see us off," he says.

"I'm going with you," she says.

"Okay."

"I have some work I need to do in Victoria, so I thought I might as well accompany you guys on the train."

Sarah stares at her. "Really?"

"Is there a problem?" Azandra acts offended.

"No," Sarah says, "it just seems like quite a coincidence."

"Well, I didn't know about it until I arrived home."

"It will be good to have another girl to talk to. Boys can be pretty boring, you know?"

"Thanks, sis." I feign hurt feelings. We all laugh which helps to relieve the tension.

At the Kinsol Trestle, we stop and Sarah quickly reminds us not to go anywhere, as she is in no mood to go looking for us again. We sit on a bench facing the south side of the bridge and stare at all of the people milling around, buying souvenirs and taking pictures.

"Do you see that man with the black cap?" Azandra whispers to me.

"Yeah. What's so special about him?"

"He doesn't fit the profile of tourist."

"Maybe he's on business," Ricky says.

"I think I've seen him before," Azandra says. "In my time, he is a guard at New Albion."

"So, he's one of Mohryia's spies?" I ask.

"Yes, I'm sure of it. Where is your sister?"

"She's still on the train. She said she was tired."

"Stay here and watch him. I'll go check on your sister."

"Okay," I say. "Ricky, I'm going to ghost him for a bit, and you watch from here." Ricky nods his head. "*Fac mihi interitum,*" I say, invoking invisibility and approach the man. He pulls out an object and talks into it.

"The magic boys are here, but the girls are on the train. Only see one of the wizards is here, don't know where the other one is."

"Be careful," a voice says from the object. "They may use magic. One of them could be invisible right now." The man looks around as if expecting me to pop up in front of him at any moment. He clicks the object off and shoves it into a pocket; then hurriedly dashes off toward the train. He heads towards Ricky, gives him a quick look and then hops on the loco motive.

"*Fac mihi apparet,*" I say and reappear beside him.

"Billy, what did you find out?"

"He's definitely working for someone other than the council, probably Mohryia. He was talking to someone using a communication device. We should keep an eye on him. He's monitoring our movements."

"We'd better tell Azandra," Ricky says. "Yeah, time to get on the train anyway." We board the train.

"Be careful," I tell Azandra when she's away from Sarah. "That spy you told us about is on the train and he might try something."

"I doubt he would be so bold with all of these passengers around. More likely he'll wait until Victoria when we leave the depot. Just in case, we should stay together as much as we can."

Later, I'm standing in front of the washroom sink when he steps in. "Quite the train, eh?" he says as he walks over to the urinal.

"Yeah, pretty cool, just like going back in time."

He gives me a strange look. "I guess it would be like that if we could," he replies.

"In the future, we'll all be flying around in spaceships. There won't be any need for ground travel like trains."

"Yes, probably. It will be a shame to give up the railroad; it's sort of fun to ride, isn't it."

"Sort of. Well, nice talking to you," I say, toss some paper towel into the garbage and head out the door. In the corridor I look at pamphlets of points of interest for Victoria from a rack. When he comes out, he glances left, right, sees me and goes in the other direction.

Billy—He's coming your way. Ricky—I'll follow him.

I stop where Sarah and Azandra are sitting and notice that we're entering Victoria depot in Esquimalt\Vic West.

Sarah appears to be sleeping so I whisper to Azandra to be ready for the spy to make a move. Then, I shake my sister. "Wake up, sleepy head. We're back in Victoria."

"What," she says and yawns while sitting up, gazing out the window to the old brick train turnstile depot. The whole building has been renovated to look like it did, years ago. Five other old locomotives are housed here as they take turns chugging up the rails of the island corridor. *What will happen to it all after the disasters in the future that Azandra has told me about? All of the historical sites must be ghost towns in her time—unless the Outlanders occupy them. That would make sense.*

Ricky comes back from his surveillance.

"Mom's there," Sarah says, and I see her standing on the platform looking for us. She looks older since dad left us. I guess it has taken a toll on her.

"Hey, you delinquents," she says, laughing, and gives us a hug as we step onto the wooden deck. "That wasn't very nice, leaving us to worry about you. And who is this?"

Azandra steps forward. "This is Azandra. We met her on the train."

"Nice to meet you," Azandra says.

"Likewise," Mom says. "Unusual eye color. It's very pretty, though. What brings you to Victoria?"

"I have business down here."

"Oh? What kind of business?"

"Travel, bookings to different places, like a special travel agent."

"What company do you work with?" Mom asks.

"Mostly freelance. Almost a hobby really."

"Really?" Mom presses.

"Actually, I must be off. Have to meet a client. Taxi!" our future traveler calls and a white electric car pulls up.

"See you later, Azandra," Ricky and I say.

"Yes, I'll call you later." She hands her luggage to the tall driver and hops into the cab. As I'm watching I see our spy walk past us and head for a waiting black SUV, just like in a movie or something. The black car quickly pulls out and follows Azandra. Why doesn't he wait to follow us?

"Well, did you get a lot of your research done?" Mom asks.

"Yeah, from Azandra's father. He was a railroad engineer on the E&N. He knew a lot of things about the old railcars and locomotives, schedules, stuff they hauled, mostly coal, and some of the famous people who traveled up and down the island."

"Glad to hear it was so successful," Mom says. "And, Sarah, you won your game. Good for you."

"Yup, and next weekend we play the Port Alberni Aces at Tyndal Park."

"Glad it's a home game so I don't have to worry about you," Mom says, smiling at her.

"I'm old enough to take care of myself, Mom."

"Yes, I guess you're getting older every year, honey, but you'll always be my baby."

"Mom," Sarah complains, but smiles back. Ricky and I laugh from the back seat.

As we turn down Lampson Street, a black SUV follows us. "Ricky, that car has been behind us for most of the way," I whisper.

"Yeah?" Ricky questions and looks around. "I don't recognize it."

"Let's see how far it goes."

When we turn right at Greenwood, it follows. "Still there," Ricky says. It follows us right to our house; slows down as we turn in and then carries on up the street.

"It didn't have a usual plate. It read 123 Tm-Trvl," I say.

"How appropriate," Ricky says.

"You guys hungry?" Mom asks.

"Starved," I say.

"Yup," Ricky echoes.

"You bring in the bags and Sarah and I will make some lunch," Mom says.

After lunch, my cellphone rings and Azandra is on the other end. "Billy, we definitely have people watching us. That guy from the train followed me to my apartment."

"Yes, well, we had a black SUV follow us to our door. His license plate read 123Tm-Trvl."

"That makes sense. They must be part of Mohryia's group. Be careful. I will come and pick you two up in an hour, okay?"

"Okay. Should we meet you somewhere instead of the house just to throw them off?"

"Yes, could you walk down to Saxe Point Park?"

"Sure," I answer. "Where do you want to meet?"

"Don't worry, I'll find you. It's safer that way."

The sun was shining with a slight breeze blowing like always. This park was my childhood hangout. I love this place; the trees, waves against the rocks and the sea life. Ricky and I walk down the path that takes you to the cove on the right side. "Remember when we were little, Ricky, and we followed those smugglers with the trunk?"

"Oh, yeah. You almost got caught because your bike died." He laughs.

"Yeah, that was close. We didn't even know anything about magic back then," I say as I watch an eagle land up on a tall fir tree.

"Yes, things have sure changed," Ricky says. "It would have been different if we knew what we know now, back then."

"I guess that's part of growing up, man. At least we've learned a lot since then, like how to deal with evil entities. I wonder how much this Mohryia knows about magic?"

"He knows enough to travel in time and destroy a lot of good people. If he's responsible for the destruction caused by WW III, he must be pretty powerful," Ricky says.

"We'd better make sure that we have all of our spells ready and keep our reflexes sharp."

"I think that we should stay together too. We're more powerful that way, like when we fought Dobbins at Lampson School."

"What about Sarah? I have a feeling that we're not going to be able to keep her out of it."

"Yup, knowing her. What if we told her about it?
She might be safer if she knows what's going on."

"What if she freaks out?"

"Let's ask Azandra first. She might be able to help, and Sarah will be more likely to believe it if it comes from her."

"Speaking of future girl, there she is by that tall oak tree, coming our way."

"Hey, boys. Let's just keep walking for a while," she says, passing us slowly.

"We need to talk," I say.

"Let's go a little deeper into the woods where we have privacy." Ricky and I follow her where she stops on the other side of a small pond nestled around several tall trees and bushes. Crows are squawking up in the trees and two young deer are drinking at the pond. I feel the peace and beauty around me and re- member my childhood.

"Okay, we need to start our search for Mohryia and his henchmen," Azandra says.

"Yeah, but do you have any leads," I ask.

"As a matter of fact, one of my agents just told me that Mohryia is in Victoria meeting some foreign agent."

"Do you know where they're meeting?" Ricky asks.

"And when?" I ask.

"No, just that it's somewhere in Esquimalt."

"Okay, where's your car?" I ask.

"I've rented a vehicle. Follow me." She turns and heads along the path.

As we catch sight of the roadway I say, "Azandra, we need to talk about my sister."

She stops and turns to face us. "Sarah? What about her?"

"We're both worried that if we don't tell her about this, she might be in danger without being aware of it," I say.

"She is a little young to deal with it," Azandra says as we reach the roadway.

"Maybe, but she has an insight that keeps her aware of danger, and she might be able to help us, too."

"How can she help?"

"She has visions and may be able to tell us where Mohryia is."

"Really?"

"Yes."

"She probably already is aware of some of this," Ricky says.

"Yes, I am." My sister steps up from behind us.

"Sarah," I say.

"Well, Sarah, I guess you're not going to let us keep you out of this, are you?" Azandra says. "Let's not tell your mom though. I don't think she needs to be worrying about you, okay?"

"No problem," Sarah says. "Now, if we're going to catch up with this Mohryia guy, we'd better hurry."

"You know about him?" Ricky asks.

"Yeah, I was pretty sure about it in my last dream when Billy was fighting him," she says.

"What?" I say. "I was fighting him?"

"Yeah, that's why I thought I should find you guys and tell you before he disappears."

"Disappears?" Azandra says. "What do you mean?"

"If you want to catch him, I know where he is."

"Where?"

"In the restaurant at the mall on Esquimalt Road," Sarah replies. "Let's go before he's gone."

At the café, we wait in the car and after about five minutes, two men come out who Azandra says are Mohryia and one of his cohorts. The wizard looks tall with long black hair, black eyes and a Fu Manchu. He's wearing a black vest over skintight black leather pants. His arms are covered in tattoos of skulls, snakes and dragons. His eyes flash in our direction and, for a second, I think he's spotted us, but then his attention is distracted by a limousine that slides quietly beside him. A woman pops out and opens the passenger door for him. We watch as he disappears out of the lot.

"Quick, follow him," I say to Azandra, who steps on the gas and boots the rented Mustang into gear. We chirp out of the parking lot and spin into the street about three cars behind him.

"What're we going to do when we catch up to him?" Ricky asks.

"Well, I'm relying on your magical expertise to figure that out," Azandra says. As we watch the wizard's car, it speeds up with blue sparks surrounding it.

"Keep close, Azandra," I say. She changes lanes and speeds past the car in front of us and then swerves ahead of the next car to end up right behind Mohryia's. It turns a corner to the right and we follow in hot pursuit, but it suddenly bursts ahead, flickers, and disappears in a cloud of blue haze. We zoom right through the mist left behind, but the black vehicle is gone.

"Damn, where did they go?" Azandra asks as she pulls over to the curb and stops.

"Any feeling?" I ask Sarah.

"Yes, but they're not in our time anymore. I can't sense them," she says.

"Well, I guess we missed them," Ricky says. "What do we do now?"

"We go back to my agent. He might know where they've gone," Azandra says. She wheels around the street and heads back to Esquimalt Road. About a half hour later we arrived at the train station. As soon as we park, a short, hefty man wearing a ball cap, t-shirt, and jeans comes over to the car. We step out and Azandra addresses him. "We missed Mohryia," she says. "He eluded us by traveling through time."

"Yes, he's done that several times," the agent says.

"I think he's in the past," Sarah says.

"What makes you say so?" Azandra asks.

"I can sense somewhere that I've been before, somewhere along the E&N Railway line.".

"Where?" I ask.

"Near the trestle, I think."

"That would make sense," Azandra says. "That's where one of the portals is located."

"But, why would he go into the past?" I ask.

"We won't know unless we find him," Azandra says.

"How do we do that?" Ricky asks.

"What do you think, Sarah? Can we locate him on the time continuum?" I ask.

"I think I can, but I have to be at the trestle to sense him because that's where the portal is."

"It will take a long time to drive to it or take the train, unless I activate the disk," Azandra says.

"We've got a faster way," I say. "Right Ricky?"

"Yes, through another portal close by," he answers. "There's one on the top of the hill at Beacon Hill Park."

"Let's go then," Azandra says. "Roger, you stay here and keep in touch with home base."

"No problem." The agent steps away from the car. We spin out and head toward the downtown park.

— CHAPTER SEVEN —

Dragon Eyes

"Everyone, hold hands," I say as we stand by the flag at the top of Beacon Hill. I sweep my wand over us. "*Nos ad Kinsol*." For a moment, we see the sky and feel the wind, then just as quickly we arrive at the Kinsol Trestle. Luckily, the train is not present because we land right on the bridge.

"Ah!" Sarah exclaims as we stagger to our feet. "Did you have to be so exact, Billy?"

"Sorry," I answer, "but we can't always land safely. You have to be ready for anything when magic is involved."

"Sarah, can you sense them?" Azandra says, bringing us back to the task at hand.

"Let me see," my sister says. She holds her arms aloft and twitches her fingers.

"Well?" our purple eyed girl says, her hands on her hips.

"Give me a minute." Sarah turns around and closes her eyes. "Yes, I feel their presence, but they're definitely in the past somewhere. I see a man with paint on his face. He has long fingernails and wears an oriental costume, like Chinese people do at ceremonies. I also see a dragon with red eyes, green scales and golden talons."

"It sounds like Chinese sorcery," Azandra says. "Who else do you see?"

"I see Mohryia. He's chanting something."

"What's he saying?" Ricky asks.

"I can't make it all out. *Draconi*, something?"

"Ricky! He's invoking a dragon!" I say.

"Yes, but to what end?"

"Indeed," Azandra says. "Can we stop him?"

"Not from here. We have to be in his time to affect him," I say.

"Well," says Azandra, "let's follow him into the past."

"I need the 'Leo' or 'Ocular orb' like in our fight against Dobbins at Lampson School, to do that," I say.

"We need to go get it," Ricky says.

"Where is it?" Azandra asks.

"Back in my bedroom," I say.

"Why can't we just travel through the portal after him?" Azandra asks.

"If we tried, we might not end up there without a guiding source like the orb," Ricky says.

"Yeah, it would be a bummer if we ended up years away from him and you never know where you're going to land without guidance," I say.

"We could find ourselves in the middle of an ancient battlefield or somewhere worse." Ricky adds.

"Let's transport to the house, get the orb and come back."

"If there is no other choice, let's go," Azandra responds.

After half an hour or so, which includes lying to mom, we're back at the Kinsol Trestle looking at the river below, listening to the rushing white water and the eagles soaring above.

"Hold hands," I say as I concentrate on the Leo in my hand. "*Panthera*." The orb clears like crystal. I focus my thoughts on Mohryia and repeat the invoking words. "*Panthera, Panthera, Panthera.*"

Almost immediately our surroundings disappear, and we're sucked into the ether. Sarah starts as I grip her hand tightly. The swirl of colors only lasts for seconds, and we are deposited on a dirt pathway beside a river rolling noisily over the rocks. "Everyone okay?" I ask as I put the Leo in my jacket pocket.

"What time are we in?" Sarah asks.

"Not sure, but we are definitely in the past," Ricky says,

"Look." He points down the path we're on to where a first nation's person, dressed in animal hide is leading a horse. A rifle sticks out from the saddle.

"Duck," I say as the man turns toward us. He gazes as if expecting someone to come down the path from above us. "Get off the path," I whisper, almost shoving my sister into the bushes. We hear horses and voices above. I can't make out the words, but we huddle out of sight as four native people pass us and join up with the leader. He has a headdress made of eagle feathers and they wear moccasins on their feet. "Probably late 1700's or 1800's," I say.

"Well, we're at least one hundred and fifty years in the past," Azandra says.

"I sense him up the trail," Sarah says.

"Good, because I wouldn't want to go the other way and try to explain who we are to the First Nation's people," Ricky says.

"Be careful. There may be others up ahead," Azandra cautions.

"I'll scout ahead," Ricky says and skips in front of us.

"Wait a bit," I say as Sarah starts after him. We watch him jog ahead until he's out of sight over the ridge of the hill above. "Okay, let's follow slowly." I lead the girls and we're soon on top of the ridge.

"Stay low," Ricky says as he points towards the small valley in front of us. We see a large hole in a rock face on the other side of the valley that has been recently blasted out of the rock. Railroad tracks creep up to it from a bridge which spans the river. Tents rest beside the tracks. Men in traditional Chinese clothes walk in and out of the tents and the hole above.

"They are railroad workers from long ago," Sarah says.

"Yes," Azandra says, "but where is Mohryia?"

"And what is he doing here?" I ask.

"He's in the second tent," Sarah says.

We cautiously travel halfway across the valley until we reach some piles of rock. As we watch a dark cloud above us forms and lightning crackles out of it striking the ground all around the tents.

"Let's find some cover," Azandra says.

"Over there," I cry as another clap of thunder follows a slash of fire from the sky. We ran to a space between the blasted rock piles in front of the cave. There we are met with about a dozen Chinese railway workers all huddled together. We overhear them talking but we don't understand them. That is until Azandra starts conversing with them. *I guess Chinese is important to know in the future.* After a bit of chatter by her and two of the men, I notice them shake their heads in agreement.

"It's okay," Azandra says to us, "they think we are travelers from Europe, with strange clothes and accents; nothing to worry about."

"Good," I say, and Sarah and Ricky nod in agreement. "That will make it easier to deal with them.

"Yes," Azandra says, "and harder for Mohryia to sway them against us."

The dark cloud above us flashes with terrible brilliance and from within it a silver dragon bursts forth. It rumbles a fierce sound, belching fire over our heads.

"*Draco, contra eos!*" Someone shouts from behind the descending creature. We look over the boulders and see Mohryia standing with a sparkling wand in his hand. A purple bolt of energy spirals up from him and surrounds the dragon, which immediately flashes its yellow, glowing eyes in our direction. "*Impetus!*" the evil wizard shouts. The dragon opens its huge jaws, breathes in, and snorts a torrent of blue flame at us.

I stand and face the beast, wand in hand. "*Declinet ignus!*" I shout, my hands forming a bluish protective field around us like a bubble.

"*Duratis!*" Ricky yells, sending blue streams of energy from his wand, at Mohryia.

"*Sicubi incantatores!*" Mohryia shouts, and the blue energy dissipates around him. "*Dolorem!*" He creates a fiery bolt with his hands, hurling it at us.

I just have time to say, "*Sicubi incan...*" before the red electricity strikes. I've diluted it but not stopped it and the pain charges through me, knocking me to my knees.

"Ricky! *Panthera!*" I yell as the dragon circles for another attack and Mohryia rotates his wand cre- ating a massive ball of red energy. "*Panthera! Panthera! Panthera!*" we yell together, wands sparking. The earth vacillates. We grab the girls by their arms and disappear into a spiraling tunnel.

— CHAPTER EIGHT —

Outlanders

In a few moments, we are spiraling down onto a field of snow. We roll over the sea of white and end up a jumbled mess at the edge of the blanket of cold crystals, looking up at fir trees appearing more like ice cream cones. I notice the wind is blowing mercilessly and realize we must be in the future near New Albion.

"Welcome to the future," Azandra says.

"I was wondering," Sarah says. "Why does it feel like winter?"

"Because the world is in a new ice age," I tell her.

"What?" She shakes the snow off her and shivers. "How did that happen?"

We explain to her how the apocalypse occurred, World War III and the resulting weather outcome.

"Where do you live?"

"In a giant globe," Azandra says. "Let me call for help and I'll take you there." She touches a button on her arm and a hologram of a soldier appears above it. "This is Azandra, number 215906, requesting assistance at these coordinates. Please send an orb, ASAP."

"Your request has been acknowledged," the man in a soldier's uniform says. "It should be within a half hour or so, Commander."

"Hurry, as we are in hostile territory."

"Find shelter and we'll be there ASAP, over and out."

Azandra turns off the image by touching her arm. "Well, let's get out of the open."

"We can huddle over there inside that grove of trees," Ricky says, pointing to our right.

Suddenly, a burst of bright yellow flashes over our heads. We jump in Ricky's direction, but freeze as someone yells, "Stay where you are or you'll be disintegrated!"

Turning, I can see four or five beings aiming rifle-like weapons at us and advancing quickly.

"We have no weapons!" Azandra says as she raises her arms in submission. We all follow suit.

"You trespass on Outlander territory," says the one who yelled as he lowers a scarf from around his face. I can see scars on his cheeks where his scruffy red beard does not cover. He snorts and spits in the snow. "Albion freaks. If you weren't valuable to my leaders, I would cut you down where you stand." He pushes his weapon towards us, as do the others. A yellow energy smelling of sulphur wafts from the tips of the barrels. "Tie their hands, Lowdy," he tells a short, stumpy man, who lumbers forward along with a slender comrade, and they tie our hands. "Now march!" the leader shouts at us.

Azandra moves forward as she gives a look that says, *Just do as they say and we'll find a way out of this.* We walk for what seems like miles through a valley where we can hear odd animal sounds and the beating of wings followed by intense squawking.

"A Fireraptor, Spanner," Lowdy says.

"Under the trees!" the leader shouts, and we all jump below the branches of tall firs. Shivering, we look out into the snowy sky. "Keep quiet and we may escape the wrath of the death bird."

Our captors aim their weapons toward the sky as we huddle like mice under a rock. The shrill cries of the Fireraptor get closer and closer until we wish we could cover our ears. Then the sky darkens, and a revolting smell assaults our nostrils. A cry so loud it makes my head throb, pierces our minds. A roaring crack assaults us next as the top of one of the trees crashes around us.

"We are doomed," one of the men says.

"Then, we will bring it down with us," Lowdy says, stepping out and aiming above. A mighty swish and a giant pair of claws picks him up, his screams rising above us. His weapon falls useless by the tree.

"Let us face this beast," I say to Spanner. "We can use magic."

As I say this another tree crashes to the ground. "Release them," Spanner says, his weapon aimed at us now.

"Ricky, together."

"Right," he says, and we both aim our wands at the soaring black beast above us.

"On three, ensnare the bird...one...two...three! *Deceptus Raptor!*" We both send a bolt of blue energy at the squawking beast as it descends toward us.

"*Deceptus Raptor!*" we shout again and watch as the blue fire encircles the huge beast, trapping its sharp claws and pinning its wings closed causing the smelly behemoth to spin into a death spiral. Ricky and I dart back under the protection of the branches as it falls just meters away from us. The snow flies up in a cascade and buries us while the ground shakes with the thunder of its fall.

"Okay," Spanner says. "Let's move before its mate catches up with us."

We travel through the valley until we come across a waterfall. One of the men leads us around the water and underneath it where there's a cave. Inside, nothing but darkness, except for lit torches on the walls which reflect the activities of several inhabitants all dressed like our captors, in ripped wraps of furs and clothing. The smell is putrid, something be- tween a men's locker room and dead fish. Many of the inhabitants have sores and scars on their faces as if from burns. Down a back tunnel the walls open up to a grand underground cavern at least fifty feet high and more than a mile across. It is light, seemingly lit up by the rock itself.

"Phosphorescence," Azandra says as we are told to stop and stand before a throne-like seat cut out of the rock. I notice that spaces are gouged out of the walls allowing for living areas where families are walking about as if this is a big village. In the distance, I can see a few more waterfalls and a river. Further down the tunnels the space opens up to bushes and fields with various food plants. It's like a secret underground world. The energy from the rocks must supply light for them so photosynthesis can occur.

A man steps up to the throne and sits. He's wearing a headdress that sort of reminds me of the First Nations' people from the past. It's made of feathers as well, but they are all black like the

Fireraptors. He has red paint on his face and chevrons on his blue coat jacket resembling sergeant stripes on an old civil war tunic.

"Welcome to the Outlander city of Light, Albion freaks. I am Sergeant Striker, Leader of the Light. Why do you trespass on our land?" He snorts and spits.

"Gross," Sarah whispers.

"Shh!" I caution her.

"Sergeant Striker, I assure you we had no intention of trespassing," Azandra says.

"More likely spying on us," our captor leader says.

"Quiet!" Striker says. "Let her speak."

"Thank you. We unfortunately got caught in a storm and lost our path, sir. We have no weapons or reason to harm anyone and wish to go back to New Albion."

"Yes, well," Striker says, "I would be happy to oblige, but then you will report back to your soldiers, where our city is and they will come and destroy it."

"You have my word as a member of the Galactic Council..."

"Hush! Your word has no weight here, Albion witch. You are valuable as a hostage, and we will keep you to ensure no hostilities befall us by your fickle councils and alien agendas." He spits the words at her. "Take them to the lower cells, but do not harm them...yet! Save them for the wizard. He'll know what to do with them."

We are led down several dark tunnels to a pit below the city where there is little light. They lock us in a cell with bars on the door.

"If you're lucky we'll feed you," our nasty Outland captor says as he slams the door shut and locks it. His fellow guard laughs.

"What can we do now?" Sarah asks, tears forming. Our captor laughs and leaves us with one guard watching.

"Wait, get fed, then form a plan to escape," Azandra whispers. "Boys, can you do magic down here?"

"I don't know," Ricky says.

"We'll try something easy and see if it works," I say. "Block the guard's view," I whisper to Ricky and Sarah. They move in front of the cell bars and Azandra adds her body in between.

"*Ignis*," I say into my cupped hands while facing the back of the cell. I feel heat but no fire ignites. Looking around the cell I located a pile of straw-like material, presumably for a bed. I pick some up and focus. "*Ignis.*" This time a small flame appears in my hand and the straw burns. "*Ignis desino.*" The fire goes out. I wave the smoke away. "It works," I whisper to the others. "Did the guard notice?"

"What's that smell?" The guard's question answers mine. We don't say anything as he sniffs and walks around the cell. "Were you burning something?"

"No," Azandra says. "How could we? We have no fire."

"Something was burning," the scruffy man with long black hair snorts at us, looking intently through the bars. "You," he points at me. "You did something!"

"How could I?"

"You used magic." He reaches through the bars trying to grab me. I jump away from his grasp. "I know you did something," he mumbles, scratching his head, and then leaves the cell area.

"Can you do anything else?" Azandra asks.

"Yeah, bro, like get us out of here," my sister says.

"Maybe, if we work together. We're not as powerful without our wands," Ricky says, raising his eyebrows.

"Let's give it a shot," I say. "How about trying to send Azandra to New Albion? That way we could try sending Sarah next, then, maybe even ourselves."

"Sounds good," Ricky says. "Azandra, stand between us." She steps forward and Ricky and I both focus.

"*Mittet in eam, New Albion*," we chant together. As we watch, a wind swirls between us and Azandra is wrenched from the cell and disappears.

"Okay, Sarah, now you," I say, but before we can enact the spell again, the guard comes back with the Outlander leader.

He aims his weapon at us, the yellow light emanating slightly.

"Stop! Or I will melt you!"

Sarah makes the decision for us by jumping away. "Okay, okay," she says, "just don't hurt us."

By this time the other guard has opened the cell. "Put them in separate cells and chain them in," Striker says, "And where is that Albion witch?"

— CHAPTER NINE —

Mohryia

They put us in a separate cell chained to the back wall. The light from the torches flickers in my face as I try to think of a way out of this. "Ricky, can you move at all?"

"No, there is some strange blue energy containing me," he replies.

"Billy," my sister says in a trembling voice, "I can't feel my arms, hands, or face. I'm scared."

"Try to be calm," I tell her. "It won't help to be emotional. You'll just use up your strength."

"Quiet," Ricky warns, "I hear someone coming."

I look over by the stone stairs and watch a guard holding a torchlight proceed a hooded figure. As the guard steps aside, I see the person lower the hood and shake his long black hair.

"These are the prisoners," the guard says, waving the torch in our direction.

"Open the doors," Mohryia commands. He raises his arm, a wand in his hand, blue light sparking from it as he smiles at us. "Ah, we meet again, young wizards. Surely by now you realize how useless your attempts at stopping me are. You have aligned yourselves with the wrong society. The New Albions and others of the Galactic Council choose to control the future. We, the Outlanders, choose to control our own destinies. Join us and you will be granted more power than you have ever wielded."

"You lie," I say. "You're the one who chose to control the events of the future with your manipulation of past events. You caused WW III and the Ice Age which followed."

"You will find that those past events were not my doing. The Galactic Council has deceived you so that they can use you to try and stop me. The truth is we are the freedom fighters, but if I cannot convince you, we will have to destroy you." He smirks at us and the guard laughs.

"Will you give us a chance to make up our own minds?" Ricky asks.

"If you do not believe the councilors, why do you do their bidding?" Mohryia asks.

"We are caught in the middle of your battle with the New Albions. We have not heard your side, but we are willing to listen," I say.

The dark wizard wrinkles his brow and scratches his beard. "Alright, boy, we will allow you some leeway, but the first sign of treachery and you shall pay for your deception. I will not tolerate falsehoods. Do you understand?"

"Yes, of course," I say. Ricky and Sarah nod their heads.

"Guards, bring them to the sacred hall, but keep their restraints on for now." He quickly spins on his heel and is gone in a pillar of black smoke.

"Quite the exit," Ricky says.

"Are you surprised?" Sarah says.

"Not really," Ricky says as the guard unlocks each cell and we are led up the stone steps and along a dark hallway, but not back to the throne room. Instead, we are taken to a large room with an open fire in the middle. There are posts surrounding the fire pit. Each one has its own chains and handcuffs, which we are immediately attached to. Sarah whim- pers as we are left hanging from the pillars, our bodies feeling the intense heat from the flames.

"Billy! Do something!" she cries.

"Try to calm down," I tell her. "We have to hope that Azandra is figuring something out." I try to sense magical forces around me, but to no avail.

--*-*-*

"But I know they are in the underground city," Azandra argues with the council members surrounding her.

"Yes, but as you also know, we cannot just enter that realm without facing Mohryia's magic, and if we give up our advantage we are lost," Rhunella says.

"If only we could communicate somehow with the boys," Arnon says.

"We can." Rodan stands and addresses the council. "Our species has the ability to use telepathy and find their energy. I will bring in Bhinder. She is our most powerful sentient."

"Yes, send for her right away," Rhunella says.

Rodan reaches into his vestment and pulls out a red crystal panel, placing it in front of him on the table. He sits, closes his eyes, and speaks softly. As he repeats certain tones like musical notes, an image of a woman's face appears on the panel. She has the alien features of Rodan, but she is slight with long red hair and green eyes. Her pale grey skin looks like it doesn't belong with the rest of her features, but such are the Grey Hybrids.

"Rodan. You wish to speak with me?" Bhinder asks.

"Yes, as the strongest seer of our colony, we need you to locate the two magical wizards," he says, still sitting, trance-like. Bhinder's face fades in and out as she focuses. Slowly, a picture appears of the room with the fire and the pillars.

"Where are they?" Rhunella asks.

"In the Outlander city below ground," Bhinder answers.

"Can you communicate with them?" Rodan asks.

"Yes," she says, then fades in and out again. "Boys." Azandra and the others watch in fascination as Bhinder's voice rises. "Boys, I am Bhinder of the Grey Hybrid race."

"Who?" Billy asks.

"Where are you?" Ricky asks. All three of them look around.

"Who are you talking too?" Sarah asks, pulling at the chains, her wrists bleeding slightly with the effort.

"I am Bhinder," the grey alien says. "I am with you and will help you."

"How?" Billy asks, shaking his chains in anger.

"Know that the council is meeting and channeling their energy to you, through me. If you focus on my eyes, you will feel the force of our efforts. We cannot free you, but we can surround you in protective energy."

"I do feel as if something is holding me up," Sarah says, after several minutes.

"Yes," Bhinder says. "Just let it envelope you and cease your struggling. We are with you." The door opens to our left and Mohryia enters. Bhinder's face disappears.

"Well, time travelers; are you ready for some evidence?" Mohryia waves his arm, and a huge screen appears against a wall. "This is a historical memory from the Archive of the Antiquities presented to you from the race of the Dagon, who are a reptile species which came to Earth millennia ago. They have been living below the oceans in domed cities from before the ascent of man and have no reason to twist the real events of the past."

We watch as a green alien appears. He has lizard- like skin, slitted, heavy-lidded eyes and a bony ridge at the top of his skull looking a little like a pompadour. His suit is dark with the appearance of an outside layer of skin, somewhat leatherish and covering his torso down to his feet. Black boots enclose them. He waves his hand over a panel in the video stream and a visual record runs showing world events; the North Korean nuclear crisis of 2025, China's devastation and subsequent retaliation, the attack on Israel by Iran, Russia and Afghanistan, WW III and the advent of the Ice Age.

"As you can see, I was not directly responsible for the cataclysm of events. If anything, the nations' own greed, suspicion and arrogance caused most of the tipping effects that changed the world's climate, not mine. In fact, I tried to stop the destruction by warning the nations of their continued aggressiveness and the consequences it would lead to." The pictures change to show Mohryia talking to delegates of the United Nations of the time.
"...and furthermore, your continued acts of aggression will undermine alliances and lead to the fall of all nations and the destruction of mankind..."

His evidence is quite convincing, I'm thinking as the pictures continue, leading up to the present state of affairs, ending with Rhunella's denial of the Galactic Council's involvement in the destruction of the world order of 2055, when the Outlanders broke away from humanity to forage alone in the wilds of the frozen environment of the new ice age.

The images stop and Mohryia waves his hands to turn down the flames in the pit. He then sends a cooling breath of fresh air in our direction. "As I've shown you, I was not responsible for the destruction of our world. Mankind's own greed and distrust led us to the brink. If anything, I tried to stop it."

"It would appear that way," I say. "Although we don't have very much information to go on, I'm more likely to believe you if I can hear it from the Dagon themselves."

"This can be arranged, but you must understand my mistrust, therefore, you will have to stay contained until I can make that happen."

"What? Here?" Sarah complains.

"No, not here. I will allow you to reside in one of the guest residences. But, know that I will be monitoring you." He orders the guards to take us to our 'guest' chambers. For being underground they are surprisingly well equipped with the necessary amenities, even separate showers and baths which take advantage of the underground hot springs.

After our ablutions, we are invited to a feast, where all of the dignitaries belonging to the Outlanders' society are seated around a large table.

"We freely offer you our bounty," an old woman with grey hair and green eyes says. She wears a purple shawl over a blue dress that looks like satin and white shoes, more like ours from the past. Her gold earrings sparkle and she plays with them as she smiles. Sergeant Striker snarls, but doesn't comment. "I offer you my words as evidence of our demise," she says, "for I was a part of the Albion society at one time: before the great freeze. I am Phesia. My title was Chancellor of the Canadian Lands, and I resided in the once beautiful city of Vancouver. After the fracturing of the continent into four regions, my city was destroyed by earthquakes and tidal waves along with Seattle, Portland and Los Angeles. What was left in the west became known as New Albion."

"Why did you leave the Galactic Council?" I ask.

"We had no choice. The Greys and the Mutant Humans would not allow us to develop on our own. Their continued interference in our society forced us to leave the safety of the domes and we struck out into the wilderness where we can live and die as we see fit; not governed by the galactic races, which would enslave us, making us subservient to their wishes and control."

"How did they control you?" Ricky asks.

"We were not allowed to hunt and fish freely as we always had in the past. Their idea of nutrition is synthetic food irradiated with chemicals and nutrients added by their food and health overseers."

"We were told that the intervention of these processes was necessary to guarantee the purity of the species that survived the cataclysms," I say.

"Rather, they were to separate our kind, the so-called flaws of our genetics were to be eradicated, to make us docile, robotic mandarins to do their bidding!" Phesia says.

"So, you just walked away from the safety of the cities?" Sarah asks.

"There was no freedom for us there. We had no choice but to find our own way in the wilderness, and we have survived the harsh reality of the environment on our own!" she says, smashing her fist on the table to emphasize it.

"Yes!" several of her comrades cry in support.

"If we believe you, will you allow us to travel back to our own time and stay out of this war?" Ricky asks.

"Since your interference, it is difficult to believe your words. We will consult with Mohryia and other rulers of our race to determine your fate. Also, the Dagon will need to speak with you directly. Be patient, young ones. These are difficult decisions, and you must weigh all of the circumstances before you make the correct one. We will be patient with you and allow you the time you need. In the meantime, join us in food and enjoy our hospitality."

— CHAPTER TEN —

Azandra

"So you sit there doing nothing while the young wizards are imprisoned by the Outlanders? And what of Mohryia? Do you think he is going to release them?" Azandra addresses the Council.

"We must act carefully," Rhunella says. "If we are too hasty the wizards may be killed before we can rescue them."

"They may be killed at any time!" Azandra says, raising her fist.

"The other danger," Rodan says, "is that the wizards will be turned to their side and end up our enemies."

"Yes," Rhunella agrees, "Mohryia can be very persuasive. Years ago, he duped the nations of the world into believing he was their only hope of salvation and we all saw what became of it. He put us on the brink of extinction."

"That's why we must act now," Azandra says, raising her voice. "If we do not, all may be lost and the plan for this galaxy will be questioned again as it was when they broke away before."

"Phesia is very eloquent with her words as well. She will appeal to the young ones, especially the girl," Rhunella says. "But how can we free them without conflict, or Mohryia knowing?"

"We can use the hybrids," Rodan says. "They can sight the wizards and guide us in sending an extraction team. No weapons, no sounds, no problem."

"Bhinder," Azandra says, "can you keep a lock on all three of them?"

"Only one at a time, but there are others who can help. Two of my sisters are also high sentients, almost as capable as I am."

"We can also use phasing suits to disguise our presence," Azandra says.

"Yes, but they are not one hundred percent foolproof," Rhunella says, "and Mohryia would find them out."

"Not if we preoccupy him," Azandra says. "Some of my soldiers could fake an attack near him and draw him out."

"That would be dangerous but could work as long as we are catching Mohryia and his main soldiers unawares. Otherwise, we could still have a battle on our hands."

"Maybe, but it is better than doing nothing or waiting for the evil one to convince the wizards to join him," Azandra says.

"What does the Council think?" Rhunella asks.

"Let us take a vote on action or waiting," Rodan says.

"Okay," Rhunella addresses the group, "raise your hands if you agree with Azandra." Fifteen of the group around the table raise their hands.

"Those opposed?" Five raise their hands. "That's it then, we'll try your plan, Commander, but if anything goes awry I will disclaim the council's part in it, and hopefully stop a greater war."

"Azandra," Rodan says, "Where do you think the City of Light is?"

"We were taken along a mountain pass between two tall ice melts where the water runs, then freezes again above the flow."

"That sounds like Dragons' Run," a young soldier wearing a gold bar on his uniform says.

"Indeed," Azandra agrees.

"There are none but freakish animals there," the soldier says.

"Yes, well, that would be as good a place as any to use in defending their underground city," Azandra says. "At first light our extraction group will leave New Albion." Addressing the soldier with the gold bar, she says: "Ridges, pick your ten best and meet me by the dome launch at oh-six-hundred."

"Yes, sir." Ridges jumps to his feet and exits the chamber.

"Use all of your abilities, Azandra, and those of the sentient Hybrids. We must succeed," Rhunella says.

"I understand."

They all leave the room.

--*-*-*

"Ridges, you are late," Azandra scolds her first lieutenant.

He seems out of breath as he leads ten soldiers towards her. "I am sorry, commander, but our Intertab was late for some reason," Ridges replies.

"Truly? It is not the first time that has happened. We must be vigilant as there are spies among us and someone would have to interfere with the tab for it to malfunction."

"I sense other presences from the pod dock, Commander," Bhinder says, and her sisters nod their heads in agreement.

"Let us hurry to the pod," Azandra says. "Ridges, send your best scouts to clear the dock."

Her lieutenant signals the second and third soldiers beside him to run ahead.

"There are three entities with weapons, and they are not our soldiers," Bhinder says.

"Ridges, take two others, join your scouts and clear the pod for us."

"Yes, Commander," he says. "You and you." He taps two of his men on the shoulders and they dash forward.

"Try not to kill them," Azandra says. "We could use their intel." Her lieutenant nods his head and follows his men.

When they reach the pod dock, Azandra and the others hear cries of pain, weapons firing blue energy and three bodies lying on the dock; two are Ridges men and one is an Outlander disguised as a soldier. "What happened?"

"Two of my men were ambushed and killed before we could fire, but we shot one of them and the other two escaped using a time warp oscillator."

"How did they get that tech? Only the Greys control the TWO's," Azandra says.

"Mohryia must have gained access to the tech from the Dagon or other aliens then," Ridges says.

"We have a lot more to be concerned about then, if that is the case," Azandra says. "Our mission is of even more importance, especially if the Outlanders have gained equal footing in this conflict. We had better succeed. I fear if we don't, the young wizards will be persuaded to fight against us. Into the pods! Hurry!"

Outside New Albian the troop of rescuers leave the pods in the forest and travel through the open fields to get to the valley known as Dragons' Run. The snow has stopped, and sunlight is filtering through the grey clouds above, causing a mist to rise as the ground layer of ice thaws and releases vapor.

"Ah, the mist will help hide our presence from the Fireraptors and Dragons of the valley," Bhinder says.

"Yes, but their strong sense of smell will still find us if we are not careful," Azandra says. "We should hurry to the trees for cover." They rush to reach the shelter of the firs before they are discovered.

— CHAPTER ELEVEN —

The Dagon

"Where are you taking us?" I ask Mohryia as they hustle us into an antigravity ship larger than the disks of the Albions, but with similar abilities.

"You are going to meet the Dagon," Mohryia answers. The ship's antigrav field is boosted and we rise effortlessly above the white land around us, hover for a second in the clouds, then shoot forward at an incredible speed.

"How...how long will it take to get there?" Sarah asks, grimacing, hands gripping the seat tightly.

"Not long, little one," Mohryia says. "It is perfectly safe."

As we zip through the atmosphere, I notice we are no longer over land. The blue waves of the ocean are underneath us. I am shocked as we fly over the remains of buildings that look like skyscrapers.

"Was that a city we just passed over?" I ask. "Yes, that is the ruins of Seattle. In a moment, you will see what's left of Los Angeles." Sure enough, the next group of ruins looks even larger with some buildings still standing but scarred as if by giant swords. Great swatches are cut out of them like a huge samurai attacked them.

In the next instant, we're flying low over what I assume is the Pacific Ocean. A storm is blowing up horrific waves and there are no boats anywhere.

"Are there any sea animals left alive?" Ricky asks.

"Some, but those that survived the holocaust are not the same," Mohryia tells us.

"What happened to them?" Sarah asks.

"They are deformed and genetically altered. To escape the poisons of the sea, some developed wings and are now earth dwellers like the Fireraptors and Dragons you encountered in Dragons' Run. They feed on all life to survive."

"Are there any others?" Sarah asks, squirming in her seat.

"Many small creatures have survived like rats, badgers, wolverines and some bears that live most of their lives underground. The world is not the place you remember. The Albions and alien hybrids have destroyed it as I warned them they would."

"How much further?" I ask.

"We are over their main city now," Mohryia says. "We will enter the ocean and travel beneath it to Laundra, the Dagon city."

Our ship stops abruptly and dives into the dark water below. We slip through the depths just as easily as we darted through the air. It's as if we are in a bubble and the water separates to let us enter.

After a few minutes of travel, we see domed structures with glowing lights around them. The city spreads out on the ocean floor for miles. Over the domes, I can see other ships like ours zipping up from the depths. Dagon craft I assume.

"Do the Dagon travel in space too?" Ricky asks.

"Yes, of course, but they are fierce enemies of the Greys and the Hybrids who are trying to control our planet. Since the ice age the antagonisms between the races has escalated. The Dagon fear that the Galactic coalition will drive them from the Earth, which has been their home since before humans."

"So," I question, "Has this struggle been going on before humans existed?"

"Yes, our planet has been a breeding ground for several races, but not the Dagon. There was genetic merging with them millennia ago, but it is lost to time as most of their reptilian species were wiped out with the comet that struck the earth and erased the race of dinosaurs. The Dagon say that the Greys caused the destruction and that has sparked the animosity between them."

"Oh, my God," Sarah says, "So we are caught up in this age long battle?"

"Yes, unfortunately, but if you make the right decision to ally with us, you may have a chance to change the outcome in our favor."

"And if we don't?" Ricky asks.

"Well," Mohryia says, smiling, "hold your decision until you have met and heard from the Dagon." At this point the ship stops over a dome which subsequently opens up and we descend inside. As the water is drawn away, we see several reptilian humanoids standing before us. Our craft opens the hatch, and we step out.

"Welcome to Laundra, our most blessed city," a tall green reptile says, his voice sounding like a growl from an alligator. Several green dignitaries stand with him, all wearing tight fitting outfits complete with boots and gloves. We take tentative breaths as we depart the ship.

"These are the wizards I told you about," Mohryia says.

"Welcome," the Dagon says, "I am Tolov, leader of the Dagon people." His outfit is green as well, but he wears a purple sash like a lanyard from shoulder to hip. He presents his gloved hand to us.

"Thank you." I shake hands with him, wondering what they look like without the glove. I suppose he fears contamination from us. I notice several reptilian faces watching from windows in the structures around us.

"I understand that you wish to talk to us about the archival footage you viewed in the Outlander city," he says.

"Yes, we'd like to learn more about your existence on our shared planet," I say. Ricky and Sarah nod their heads.

"Well, follow us to the viewing room and I will have my cooks prepare a special meal while we watch the footage again and discuss it."

"Good, thank you."

We follow the Dagon receiving party along several corridors until we reach a vaulted room with many seats. The walls and the ceiling contain clear, glass-like images of several places within the city.

"Please, sit in the front and watch the video," Tolov says as he flicks a switch on a monitor at the front of the room. Instantly, the walls and ceiling turn dark and visual images reflect from all around us. We watch as the events of the recent earth changes and the current ice age flash over the room. It's like being in the middle of a movie.

"Do you have any accounts of earlier on, when the planet was young?" Sarah asks.

"Yes." Tolov waves his hand over the machine, and it stops projecting. He waves in the opposite direction and the film reverses itself. He sweeps his arm several times and the images fly by so quickly they are just a blur. Then, he slows it down and the images settle back into a comfortable viewing sequence. We see an ancient world with volcanoes erupting, and storms flashing in the sky.

"These records are of a time over 100 million years ago." Dinosaurs appear; Pterodactyls, Brontosaurs, Raptors and even a Tyrannosaurus Rex thunder by. "Now, in this next sequence you will see the precursors of your own species."

"What?" Sarah says. "You mean like apes, chimpanzees and orangutans?"

"No, before them, the earliest mammals." A picture comes up showing a squirrel-like creature with a longish snout, fur on its body, claws and a long tail. It is only about the size of a cat or small dog. "It walked the earth after the extinction of the dinosaurs, about 65 million years ago. It's quite likely that humans would never have developed if it weren't for the apocalypse that destroyed the giant reptiles."

"And you think that the Greys caused this to happen?" Ricky asks.

"Yes," Tolov replies. "Without their interference, humans would, quite likely, have developed from reptilian ancestors.

"And we would be like your race?" I ask.

"Not exactly, as every species is dependent on factors dictated by their planet of origin. We are not originally of Earth, but come from our home world, Draconus; which is only similar to Earth, as its size, gravity, atmosphere and oceans are different. Thus, we were different when we first came here, some 85 million years ago. Many of my ancestors went back to Draconus when the

K-T event occurred, but those who stayed, adapted, and survived in the oceans."

"Getting back to our concerns about Mohryia, do you agree with him about his explanation of the cause of the war and the ice age?" Sarah asks.

"As far as him being totally blameless for the demise of the 21st century civilization, no, but he is not totally at fault either. Many factors led to the destruction; human greed, escalation of weaponry, influence of various alien interests and poor decisions."

"So, part of it is his fault because he could have done something about it?" I ask.

"Yes, he could have intervened sooner and more actively, but that wouldn't have avoided it completely, only delayed it. Poor choices made by people with power cannot be stopped by magic. Also, alien agendas have affected the progress of humans since they first walked the earth. Nothing is merely chance—there are forces in the universe far greater than my efforts, which control the events of human history."

"So, it is impossible to lay blame on any one species or being's decision?" Sarah asks.

"Essentially, yes. Oversimplified, but you understand how these things work. Only, remember this, everything is done for a reason, even destruction and rebirth."

"That sounds rather fatalistic," Ricky complains.

"In a way, yes. The universe is designed, not an accident."

"So, you believe in God?" Sarah asks.

"Not as you describe in your earthly religions, but yes, there are levels of sentient involvement in the spirits of all aware intelligences in the universe."

"I guess that makes sense," I say. "So, we only have so much influence over our lives?"

"You have choice, but not the knowledge of the final design of your existence."

"Heavy," Ricky says.

"Ultimately, you must decide what you will do next. Choose carefully." With that final comment Tolov closes the video and leaves the room. Shortly after, Mohryia comes back into the room and smiles at us.

"So, have you decided who you'll support?" he asks.

"We still need time to digest all that we have seen and heard," I answer.

"It is not a simple decision," Ricky says.

"And cannot be taken lightly," Sarah adds as Mohryia stares at us with his dark eyes.

— CHAPTER TWELVE —

Dragons' Run

A Fireraptor sprays Azandra and her troops as they huddle under the firs of the valley. Branches crackle and burst under the onslaught of flame.

"Raise your weapons!" Azandra yells and dashes out into the snow, her fingers triggering the directing implants in her wrists to fire blue energy at the flaming bird above. She misses as the creature dodges the azure streams. Her fighters join her, and the death bird is struck in the snout. It screams, rears its head forward, spraying them again and flies off into the dark. One of her attack party is struck and spins around, fire flashing from his arms and chest. He yells and Azandra dives on top of him, rolling him in the snow, snuffing out the flames.

"Are you okay?" she asks, standing over him, brushing smoke and snow away from herself.

"Yes, but this helmet is useless now," he replies, throwing off the head gear, which smokes, and melts into the snow.

"Well, you're lucky to be alive. The heat alone can kill you from a Fireraptor. We need to hurry out of this valley if we are to avoid more of them."

"And we haven't even run into the Dragons yet," one of the other soldiers says. She is a tall woman with muscles almost as impressive as the male contingent of the fighters. The soldiers of the future are men, women, and alien hybrids, all working together and sharing their abilities equally.

"Yes, Ravona. Let's get moving." Azandra leads them through the trees. For several hours, they hear screams and grunts but see no raptors or dragons. They climb the final ridge of the mountain. Just as they reach the top, a dark shadow appears against the snow and a huge wingspan flies over. The shout from this creature pierces their ears as they duck under a ledge of rock jutting out from the mountain. They watch as the immense beast circles, its eyes shine orange as it focuses on them.

"Quick! Get down the mountain!" Azandra shouts and drops into the snow and foliage of the firs. Her soldiers follow her lead and dash below the safety of the trees, out of sight. The huge, scaly dragon rears up and dives, its mouth sending a ring of red fire like a giant flame thrower at the trees. The heat hits them and the trees burst and pop into fiery candle sticks overhead. "Run!"

They scramble down the ridge, a stream of burning embers following them as the huge winged lizard shrieks and continues to rain fire upon them. Two of her troops are fried in the retreat. Their screams are heard as they melt in the snow. The beast grabs them up in her huge maw, a sacrifice allowing the others to escape.

Halfway down the mountain Azandra reaches the entrance to a cave, its mouth too small for the dragon to enter. "Follow me!"

Inside the cavern, they can see strange symbols on the wall:

ДАГОН БЛУЕ СОУРЦЕ
(Dagon blue source)

"What is this?" Azandra asks. "Any of you know what language it is?"

"It looks like symbols from the old Cyrillic alphabet," Bhinder says. "Nobody speaks it anymore since the ice age."

"Obviously, that's not true as this writing is not that old. It is written with Coptic," Azandra says.

"The only burners that we know of are in New Albion," Ridges says.

"Again, we assume things, when the truth is not what we thought," Azandra says. "Someone in the Outlands has this capability. Could it be Mohryia? Or?"

"A wizard would be capable," Bhinder says, "and there may have been other Coptics that we aren't aware of."

"If that is so then information could be redirected from our mobile sectors," Azandra says. "No wonder the Outlanders know our every move. Do you know what it says?"

"No, but I may be able to find out. The Greys have a universal bank of most languages in the galaxy. I will have to connect with our space brothers to solve it."

"Good, tell me as soon as you know."

She touches her right arm and a small holo- graphic image stands on her palm. "President Rhunella, I have discovered a Cyrillic script in a cave near the Outlander city. I have reason to believe that they have been intercepting our messages for quite some time."

"How is that possible? They would need a Coptic translator."

"Mohryia may have one or he has access to one through his spies."

"That's entirely likely. He was part of the social network before they split. He had access to all digital devices, weaponry and even some alien tech."

"He also is in close contact with the Dagon, who have ancient technological knowledge; crystals, anti-grav, genetic engineering and psychic abilities."

"This battle is more complex with every discovery we make. Azandra, that is why it is so important not to make the wrong move."

"What do you mean?"

"Listen carefully, we have found out that the wizards have been taken to the Dagon underwater city. If they are turned by Mohryia, we have lost our advantage."

"I realize that, President. What do you suggest?"

"I think it would be wise to delay your intervention until the wizards have made it back to the Outlander city. Hold up where you are, and I will be in touch when I know what is happening."

"Yes, President, as you wish. We have enough supplies for a few days, but that is all."

"Okay, I will know something soon." The image disappears as Azandra turns to face her troops.

"Make yourselves comfortable. We will be here until tomorrow at least, perhaps longer."

"Commander, there is another symbol here," one of the soldiers calls out. Azandra rushes back further in the cave where a soldier is flashing his light onto more symbols:

ЦРИСТАЛ ЦОДЕХ
(Crystal Codex)

"Bhinder," Azandra says, "Copy these down as well. I need to know what they say."

"Yes, sir, I have already sent them to Rodan. He should be able to contact our language bank and get back to us soon."

— CHAPTER NINE —

Time to Think

"We'll have to go back to the underground city," Mohryia says as he herds us back to the ship. Inside, I wait for the right moment to suggest a strategy for us to escape him.

"Ricky," I whisper as we fly through the atmosphere over the ocean, which is stormy again with dark clouds and swirling seas. "We've got to find a way to transport away from Mohryia."

"I know, but how?"

"I think I have an idea," Sarah whispers to us both. "I'll zero in on a time warp signal like the one at the trestle and we should be able to escape."

"But how?" I ask. "We don't have the lion's head or any other magical device."

"Hold on," Ricky says. "These ships have teleportation devices on board. If Sarah can figure out where we need to be, maybe we can escape using it."

"Do you know where it is on the ship?" I ask.

"Yes, it's on the receiving deck when you enter or depart the ship."

"Where?" Sarah asks.

"There's a domed structure at the back of the deck."

"How do you activate it?" I ask.

"That's the difficult part," Ricky says. "When Azandra showed it to me she said the controls are set on a delay sequence from the control panel beside it. Timing is everything."

"Do you remember how to handle the controls?" Sarah asks.

"Yes, I think I can do it."

"Okay," I say, "but how are we going to get past the guards?"

"How about a diversion?" Sarah says. "I'll ask the guard over there if we can have a tour of the ship."

"Okay," I say as Ricky, and I nod.

Sarah turns to face the guard who is standing across the room. "Excuse me." The guard comes forward several steps. "Do you think it would be okay if we had a tour of the ship? It's all new to us and we're bored." She pouts.

"I will ask the wizard," the guard says.

"By that time, we'll be back at the city. Can't you just show us?" she whines.

"Hmmm," the guard sighs. "I suppose it would be okay. Alright, but any trouble and I'll freeze you." He points his weapon at us, blue energy dancing at the end of it.

"Yes, no problem," I say, holding my hands out for him to release the restraints. He clicks a button on his wrist and all of our restraints release.

"Ah, that's better," Sarah says, rubbing her arms and standing up. "Lead on, sir."

"No, you three go first where I can watch you. Turn left outside the door," he says tapping his arm and opening the door to the hallway. We proceed down a narrow hallway. The walls have a natural glow so it's easy to travel. "Turn right at the next junction," the guard says. In a few minutes, we end up at the receiving deck. We can see the ground below us and right away I recognize the E&N railcar.

"Look, guys, the train is right below us," I say, and we all look through the clear floor. "Sarah, see if you can see the trestle."

"Right," Sarah says.

"What's this dome thing?" Ricky asks and proceeds to step toward the transporter. The guard follows him and tells him about it as Sarah focuses on our drop point.

"I see the trestle," she whispers after a couple of minutes.

"Neat," I say, "I wonder how far back the train is."

"Not far," Sarah says. We watch as we see the guard open the transporter so Ricky can see the inside.

"How is it controlled?" Ricky asks.

"I can't show you that," the guard replies, standing with his back to me so it's easy for me to rush him. As I do, Ricky grabs his weapon and threatens him.

"On the ground!" he commands, and the guard drops. I wrap a restraint from his belt around his wrist, then attach the other cuff to a control panel support.

"Mohryia, the wizards are trying to escape!" the guard calls through the intercom.

"Quick!" Sarah says, "We'll be over the trestle in a few minutes." She and I hustle into the dome while Ricky sets the transporter controls. We watch nervously as he struggles with the dials and switches.

"Come on, Ricky!" I yell. "It's now or never!" At that moment Mohryia enters the deck.

"What are you doing?" he screams as he takes in the sight of the guard chained up, Ricky at the controls, and us in the dome.

"*Congelo!*" I yell just as Ricky jumps into the dome and shuts the door. My timing is impeccable as Mohryia is caught off guard. Ricky straps himself in as the dome wavers and we disappear into the ozone. The next thing we know, we've arrived back in time, but below the trestle in the cold water of the river. I grab Sarah's arm just as she is going below the surface. She comes up choking and gasping as all three of us are swept downstream by the vicious current.

"Billy!" she yells as I lose my grip on her arm. We run the rapids for several turns and twists and undertows until finally the current pauses in a tidal pool and we use the opportunity to swim to shore.

"Where are we?" Ricky asks. "More like when?" I say.

"I think we're back in our own time," Sarah says. "There's no snow on the ground and it's a lot warmer."

"Yes, you're right," I agree.

We shake the water off and look for a path or road to follow.

--*-*-*

"Finally!" Ricky says as a car pulls up beside our hitchhiking thumbs.

"What are you kids doing out here?" the driver, an older lady with grey hair and wire spectacles asks us.

"Our car broke down a way back and we don't have a cell phone, so we thought we'd better hitchhike before our parents got worried about us," Sarah says. I smile at her quick thinking.

"Well, hop in," the sweet grandmother type says, and we jump into the SUV. "Where were you headed?"

"Victoria," Ricky says. "That's where we live."

"Why were you up island?" grandma asks.

"We were there because my sister had a soccer game against the Nanaimo team," I say.

"Oh, did you win?"

"Yes," Sarah says, "but just by one goal."

When we get to Victoria, the kind old lady drops us off on the corner of Esquimalt Road and Lampson Street. In no time, we're back at Mom's house and she's surprised to see us.

"I thought you were at Ricky's house," she says, eyebrows raised. "I called but nobody answered."

"We were," I started, "but had to go do some more research at the library."

"Oh," mom says, "Why is your sister with you?"

"I was at the library too and bumped into them, so we decided to walk home together," Sarah says with a little smile.

"Well, dinner won't be ready for a few hours so you might as well do homework or whatever until then."

We head down to the rumpus room downstairs so we can talk.

"Well, what do you think we should do?" I ask. "I'm pretty sure that Mohryia is responsible for more of this future society than he's telling us. "I don't trust him," Ricky says.

"I agree," Sarah says. "He's too sure of himself. I think he has another agenda which includes power for himself. Don't forget, we went back in time and saw him using his magic to control the railway workers."

"I think he was looking for something else in the cave they were blasting, but what?" I say.

"Maybe we need to go back and investigate further," Ricky says.

"Right, we'll go tomorrow after school."

"Yes, we've got to find out what he's really up to." Sarah says.

CHAPTER FOURTEEN

A Secret Formula

"Bhinder," Azandra calls for her top sentient. "Yes." Bhinder jogs over to her commander. "I have the translation of the Cyrillic message. The first phrase says, *Dagon Blue Source*."

"Hmm, okay, what does the next one say?"

"*Crystal Codex*."

"Any idea what it all means?"

"Rodan has consulted with the Grey elders and they have told him that the Dagon have a secret formula, known as the Crystal Codex which concentrates universal blue energy for many uses, including weaponry, which, if in the wrong hands could do irreparable harm to people."

"What does that mean?"

"It means that the population would be eradicated while the environment would not be affected."

"What? Unheard of. Are you sure that's what it does?"

"The Greys know of it, but most species have agreed to ban its use."

"Why would the Dagon use it then?"

"They wouldn't, but Mohryia might."

"That must be what he's after." Azandra's communication array signals and a holograph of Rhunella appears beside them.

"Azandra, we have news that the young wizards have escaped."

"Good. Where are they?"

"We do not know, and we haven't been able to find them. The sentients have suggested that they are no longer in our time."

"They probably escaped back to their own time," Azandra suggests.

"Probably," Rhunella says. "You need to travel back and find them before Mohryia does."

"Yes, but we'll need a time pod to follow them."

"We cannot get it to you in your present location. You must leave the cave and make your way to the top of the mountain. I will send a pod there."

"A dragon was there before, that's why we entered the cave."

"Yes, well that's a chance we'll have to take. Get to the mountain top as quickly as you can."

"On our way," Azandra says and Rhunella disappears. "Ridges!"

"Yes, commander," her lieutenant asks.

"Round up our soldiers. We're going up to the top of the mountain to use a pod for transport."

"Yes, sir," he says and trots off to enact her orders.

As they reach the top of the mountain, they see no sign of dragons or Fireraptors, but they don't see a transport pod either.

"We will have to stay here until the pod arrives," Azandra says. "I don't like being exposed like this, but we do not have a choice. Everyone! Be alert for attack from above!" No sooner does she caution them when four Fireraptors zoom in from the north. "Weapons ready!" They nervously watch as the raptors near their position, screeching and howling, closer and closer. "Fire!" she yells as the raptors fly overhead. "Aim for the first two!"

Their weapons flash bluish-green overhead, but the beasts squeal and dodge the beams. As they circle around they come in closer. "Wait!" Azandra commands. "Wait until they are closer, closer, clos er...Now! Fire!"

This time the first two birds of prey are struck. They scream and spiral down on top of the clustered group of warriors who jump to avoid being struck by them. The last two raptors strike with sprays of fire and two of the troops are blasted. They scream, break ranks and roll into the scrub below. The other Albions fire but miss the birds that fly away.

"Quick, help them!" When they catch up to the wounded fighters all they can see is black, burnt carcasses. "Get their helmets off! See if they're alive!"

"They're not breathing, Commander," Ridges declares as he leans over both of them. "They're gone."

"Damn it!" Azandra yells. "Damn it to Hell!" As she curses and moans at the loss, the pod shows up overhead and alights near them. Two soldiers hop out to help, but quickly realize the worst and pick up their dead comrades. "Into the pod. Quick, before those raptors return."

"Where to Commander?" the pilot asks.

"New Albion first," she answers. "We'll catch up with the young wizards after we drop off these unfortunate soldiers."

Back at the domed city Rhunella and the Council discuss the next move for Azandra and her fighters. "We do not know if the young wizards are with us or not but it's a good bet they're not buying all of what Mohryia is selling either," Rhunella says.

"Yes, but we must be cautious," Rodan says. "If we make a move too soon, it may signal to the Dagon and the wizards alike that we are the aggressor in this battle."

"True, but if we hesitate it may be too late to save the young wizards," Azandra argues.

"You must find the wizards before Mohryia does," Rhunella says. "Go now!"

"What time setting?" the pilot asks, as Azandra and her forces sit in the pod.

"Set it to the wizards' time, 2020." In seconds, they are descending onto a hilltop somewhere near Lampson Street School. Luckily, it is surrounded by bushes and trees and not near any houses. "Bhinder, sense for them," Azandra says as they depart the pod, which disappears instantly. The hybrid sentient sits on a rock and focuses her energy.

"Well?" Azandra questions, her hands twitching.

"They are here, but their impressions are fading," Bhinder says.

"What do you mean?"

"They're travelling again. This time into the past. Hints of a railroad and a cave."

"Railroad and a cave?" Azandra echoes her. "Tell me what that means!"

"They are in the past now, the building of the railroad on Vancouver Island. North of the old city of Nanaimo. A place that was called Horne Lake."

"Why are they there?"

"I do not know, but that's where they are, about one hundred twenty-five years ago."

"Okay," Azandra says. "I'll rephase the pod and we'll go there." She touches several points on her arm and the pod appears again. "Let's go!" They pile back into the small globe and Azandra tells the pilot to reset for 1891 at Horne Lake. After several seconds, they are spiraling through time and space and ending up at a wooded area right beside a lake. They step out into what seems to be a misty scene, making it difficult to find their way.

"Bhinder, scan the wizards."

"They are not far away, in a cave to the south. Follow me."

After pushing aside brush and walking through marshy ground they come to a place beside the water where the ground has been dug out of the bank and a ten-foot cave yawns in front of them.

"They're in there but they are not alone. Mohryia is near them, but in a separate tunnel."

"Stay sharp," Azandra orders as they enter the black space.

She touches her arm and a powerful beam like a search light shows them the way forward. "Go slowly. Weapons ready, but be careful as we do not want to fry the young ones." About fifty feet back the tunnel splits left and right. "Ridges, you take three soldiers and travel left. The rest of us will go right. If you see them signal with your com." A half an hour down the tunnel Azandra stops her group and asks Bhinder to sense them again.

"They are in the other tunnel where Lieutenant Ridges is."

"Can you tell what is happening?"

"No, but all are alive."

"Turn around. We must get to them as quickly as we can."

Fifteen minutes down the other tunnel Bhinder stops them. "They are no longer together. The wizards and Mohryia are heading further down the tunnel, but Ridges' group has stopped."

"Get there as quickly as we can!" Azandra says as she hustles forward. Around a sharp turn in the tunnel they see Ridges group lying on the ground. "Oh, my God!" What happened?" Nobody answers for a few minutes.

"They're dead," Bhinder says, "all but Ridges, who is with the others."

"Follow them!" Azandra yells, and they rush after the others. After several turns Bhinder stops them again and says that the others are around the next corner.

"Slowly," Azandra whispers. "Weapons ready, follow me." She shuffles forward. At the corner a flash of energy bursts in front of them. "Back!" Two more flashes follow, and they retreat to another turn.

"Hold here," Azandra says, as she blasts two bursts of blue energy forward.

"Ah!" Someone yells from the attacking group and they stop advancing.

"Hold fast!" Azandra shouts and sends two more blasts forward. There is no response from Mohryia's group. "Mohryia!" Azandra yells. "Speak with me!" Nobody answers. Another flash comes from the turn in front of them and a wave of blue energy surges towards them knocking them flat.

--*-*-*

Azandra wakes up in the tunnel, her joints ache and her head is spinning. She looks around with her flash. All of her soldiers look dead. She checks for survivors. They are not dead, just stunned like her. She revives them.

"Where are the wizards?" Azandra asks Bhinder.

"They are outside of the tunnels. On their way to the railway."

"They're going to travel through the portal, probably to the Outlander underground city. Let's go! We still might be able to stop them," Azandra says. They race around the tunnel corners and the end appears with sunlight shining in. Scrambling up the hill they look over the top of the ridge. "Which way did they go?"

"West to the railway tracks," Bhinder says. With her small group of four soldiers and the sentient, Azandra charges along the path that leads to the railway tracks. The mist has lifted, and she can clearly see far ahead, almost all the way to the railway. A few more hills and she will see right to the trestle where the portal is. She taps her arm as she's running. "This is Azandra. Send a pod now!"

"Yes, Commander, there is one on its way. Look for it north of your current position in a few minutes," a soldier answers from New Albion.

Over the last hill, she can see the trestle and five or six figures reaching it. As she watches, a fog rises from the river below and surrounds the high structure hiding Mohryia and the wizards.

"Damn! Where is that pod!" She stops, catches her breath and looks north. As if on cue a silver pod shoots rapidly towards her and stops right in front of the group, the hatch opens and Azandra and her soldiers dash on board. "Quick, to the trestle!" The pilot zips them there in a flash, but as they descend to the tracks, they watch the figures disappear into a blue mist. "No! We're too close to lose them now. Bhinder, track them!"

"They've gone into the future. That's all. Something is blocking my senses."

"The Crystal Codex, blue energy with special qualities," Azandra says, there must have been something special in the Horne Lake tunnels. We need to go back and find it."

In the tunnels, they split up into two groups and search. After several hours of desperate searching Azandra and her group stop to refresh themselves. They eat the provisions left and drink from their pouches.

"Commander," a soldier from the other group hails her.

"Yes, go ahead," she says into her comm.

"We have come upon a sunken passage which housed something that was in a metal box."

"Is there any trace of what was in it?"

"No, but my chemscanner is picking up various rare minerals."

"Like what?"

"Element 115, 117 and a titanium-carbon hybrid substance."

"It must be the Crystal Codex the Dagon designed. Make sure you search every square inch of that tunnel area. We are on our way."

"Yes, Commander we are doing that now."

After several minutes Azandra and her soldiers reunited with the rest of their crew.

"Have you found anything else?" Azandra asks.

"Yes," a soldier says, "look at this." He hands her a pulsing, bluish-green crystal the size of his palm.

"Why is it glowing?"

"It is part of the codex crystal," Bhinder tells her. "Rodan mentioned that the glowing crystals supply a conduit for the blue energy, thus enhancing its effects. However, without enough element 115 and 117 it is ineffective."

"So, if Mohryia has both he can use it."

"Yes, but he may not have enough of each to enhance it," Bhinder says.

"We will continue to search these tunnels for more crystals and the elements. Bhinder, you will accompany me. The rest of you keep me posted on what you find. New Albion will bring you more supplies."

"Yes, Commander, as you wish," the soldier who called her answers.

— CHAPTER FIFTEEN —

Deadly Crystals

"Where are we going?" Sarah asks as Mohryia directs their travel within the Outlander ship.

"You will see soon enough," he answers. "Watch them closely."

Restrained with energy cuffs, we watch helplessly as the evil wizard leaves the bridge.

"What do we do now?" Sarah asks, struggling with her cuffs.

"We wait," I answer. "Conserve your energy. We'll need it when we get loose."

*_*_*_*_*

Mohryia lifts the metal box and places it on the bench in front of him. He smiles as he opens the lid. The crystals inside glow blue and green. He lifts them out and places each of them on a wire triad which secures them in a triangular formation. He reaches back into the box and removes two other clear boxes that appear to be contained by a wave field of some kind and places them on a small platform in the middle. A humming sound emanates from the structure in front of him.

"Are we over the city yet?" Mohryia asks, speaking into a comm box.

"Just about there," his pilot responds.

"When you are over the dome, signal me immediately."

"I will, sir," the box says back.

Mohryia's fingers tingle as he anticipates what is about to happen. He looks over to Ridges who is sitting in a chair, bound with energy cuffs. "It will be difficult for you to watch this, but if you join me and the Outlanders you may survive."

"Never, Mohryia, you might as well kill me now."

"That would be too easy. Besides, you may change your mind and be useful in my new kingdom."

"You're mad. The hybrids will destroy you before they allow this."

"It is too late for them to interfere." Mohryia turns several knobs on the control for the triad displayed in front of them. The humming gets louder and the crystals throb and pulse blue and green.

Back on the bridge, Ricky whispers, "We've got to do something."

"Maybe, if we focus, we can affect the pilot," Billy says. "Focus on him. Make him steer the ship away from the city. *Volantus ad Remotus!*"

"*Volantus ad Remotus!*" the boys say together. Even Sarah joins them in the words, hoping it will help.

"*Volantus ad Remotus! Volantus ad Remotus! Volantus ad Remotus!*" At first nothing happens as they watch the city below; in fact, they seem to be slowing down.

"Don't stop saying it," Billy says. Now they are yelling the words over and over and over.

"What?" the pilot says as he starts to steer the ship away from New Albion. "What are you doing? Stop! Stop!" Trying hard, his fingers continue the craft's direction as it turns back to where they were coming from and heads towards Outland.

"What are you doing up there?" an angry voice carries through the comm. "Turn the ship back around. Now!"

"I am trying," the pilot answers, "but the wizards...are...controlling...me..." He shakes his head and glares at us. I smile back as we continue to chant our spell.

"Damn them!" Mohryia yells. "And now the Albion fleet is after us. Keep your heading, there will be another opportunity." Several energy beams fire at us as we retreat. Most miss but one hits the ship, which bounces down and wobbles for a second before continuing its course.

"Stop chanting," I say just as Mohryia enters the room.

"Go as fast as you can," he shouts as he grabs the weapon controls and sends energy beams at the New Albion fleet. Some of them ignite, the explosions causing our ship to rock, drop and slide. Mohryia is manipulating several controls in a sequence as another blast hits us. Then we drop suddenly. "Full stop," he says.

We watch our pursuers fly right past us without firing a shot.

"Stay still until they are a few quadrants away, then take us to Outland." He turns to face us. "As for you meddling magicians, I'll deal with you back at the underground city. I'm sure Phesia will want a word or two with you as well."

"We're invisible. They didn't see us; that's why they flew past." Sarah says as we continue to watch the fleet disappear.

"Okay," Mohryia says, "take us to Outland." The pilot boosts the controls and we take off at high speed.

--*-*-*

"Commander," Rhunella asks, "What did you find at Horne Lake?"

"A crystal codex designed by the Dagon which can kill people."

"How?"

"If used in conjunction with element 115 and 117 it can wipe out all of the people living in New Albion without damaging the buildings or flora and fauna."

"Really?"

"Yes, most alien species know of it but have banned its use. The problem is Mohryia has gotten a hold of it, and he will probably use it against us."

Rhunella stares at her council members in shock.

"We must stop Mohryia before he uses this weapon," Rodan says. "I will consult the Dagon. Perhaps they know of a way to stop the Crystal Codex."

"Yes, immediately!" Rhunella says. Rodan and several other Greys and Hybrids leave the chamber with him. "Azandra, you must pursue Mohryia! Whatever it takes—use the fleet and stop him before this war is part of the past along with New Albion!"

"I'm on my way." Azandra exits the room.

In the lead ship of the fleet, Azandra and her troops are quickly approaching the Outlander territory.

"Commander," her comm lights up, "Commander, this is the tunnel group. You need to come here and see this."

"What have you found?" Azandra asks.

"Crystals and portions of the elements as well."

"Are they contained?"

"Now, yes, but it cost the life of one soldier."

"Unfortunate, but necessary to defeat Mohryia. Do not do more with it. We are on our way."

"Roger, Commander."

"Lieutenant Meyers," Azandra addresses her new second-in-command on the comm.

"Yes, Commander."

"You will stay with the fleet. Do not attack until I return. Is that clear."

"Crystal clear, sir."

With that, Azandra takes her ship through the time portal to Horne Lake. In the tunnel, the soldiers show her and the crew the crystals contained in a magnetic field at the back of a small cave.

"Bring the cases from the ship," she commands. Four soldiers, who have carried the anti-gravity containers off the ship bring them forward. They are released and guided to the back of the cave, where they float. "Open them." The soldiers activate buttons on the cases and step back. The cases open and are aligned with the containment pod in the cave. "Now, release the force field and activate the anti-gravity force." More buttons are pushed and the anti-gravs hum as the force field disappears around the crystals and element holders. The crystals and the elements are drawn slowly into the anti-gravity containers. "Close it!" With a slam the containers lock, and the deadly crystals and elements are held inert in the cases. "Take them to the ship."

— CHAPTER SIXTEEN —

Phesia

"So, you have decided to join the Albion traitors?" Phesia spits the words out. "Did you listen to the Dagon?"

"Yes," I respond, flexing my energy bonds in frustration. "But he told us that Mohryia was partly responsible for the destruction of the old world."

"Well, in truth, we were all responsible, but it is what the New Albions have done since that turns us from that path. We would lose our identity and just become automatons like their soldiers. No longer having choice, our God given right." Phesia holds her staff over her head, the blue crystal within shining brightly. Her eyes widen as she continues. "You do not know what it is like to not have control over your own destiny, never to be able to speak your mind for fear of incarceration, and their prisons are not like anything you would know of." She shudders, obviously, the voice of experience.

"Okay," I say, "but we're not the reason for your distress or current condition. Why should we be held accountable for things beyond our control?"

"True, young one, but you are willing to continue with this injustice. You are not seeing everything in its true light." She waves her staff, closes her eyes, and focuses the energy from the crystal on the far wall. Images appear of fire and torture, dungeons and hollow faces of naked prisoners crowded in dank cells, crying, bleeding...dying.

"Was that what happened to you?" Sarah cries, tears trickling down her cheeks.

"That's horrible," Ricky says. "Why would they do that to you?"

"To break our spirit and force us to accept their social dictates. If it had not been for Mohryia we'd all be dead by now!"

"So true, so true," some of the congregation echo the sentiment.

"Yes, but Mohryia is willing to kill a whole city and probably more to end this struggle," I say. "There must be another way to reason with the Albions."

"Haven't you all seen enough death and destruction?" Sarah says. "All you will accomplish is the end of the human race."

"Don't you see, or has this end been predetermined by the alien influences on this planet?" Ricky says.

"Maybe this is what the Greys and the Dagons have wanted all along. Did you ever think of that?" I say.

"That's preposterous," Phesia says, "This is a battle between humans not aliens, they're just taking sides, have ever since our existence."

"Even if that is true, do you really believe Mohryia is right in eradicating the Albions?" Sarah asks.

"If that is what it takes. It is them or us now." Phesia slams her staff onto the cave floor. "Take them from my sight. They are still blind to the Albion mind tricks." We were seized by Outlander soldiers and dragged away.

"You're making a mistake!" I yell as we leave the great hall.

"You're the ones who have made a mistake," one of the guards says. The others laugh and we are taken to a cell and locked up again. Sarah starts crying and Ricky is cursing as we wait in desperation.

"Sarah, try to be strong," I say. "We won't help ourselves by giving up."

"I know," she says, "it's just so frustrating when people are so pigheaded."

"It's not surprising though, considering what they've been through," Ricky says. "I wonder how we would feel if it had been us going through that hatred, pain and torture."

"Well, maybe so, but our concern now is getting ourselves out of this," I say. "Let's spend our energy finding a way before they kill us too."

After a few hours of waiting, we can hear a commotion above us. Explosions and rumbling shake the cave enough to reduce the stairs and tunnel into a pile of rock. Another blast causes half of the ceiling to come down and it disrupts the energy cuffs which release us.

"We need to get out of here, now!" I yell as we cough and choke on the dust and ash all around us. "Ricky, we need to find a portal. Sarah, can you sense one, I can't."

"I'll try, but this disruptive energy is interfering with my probing." She searches for a place where she can sense a time shift.

"Not in here. We need to get out of the cave."

"How are we going to do that?" Ricky says. "Not up the stairs."

"Quick! Come this way!" someone hollers from the back of the cells. We look over and see Phesia beckoning us with her hand. "Hurry, I can only hold it open for a few more minutes." She holds her staff with its blue crystal aimed at the wall behind her. We rush over and enter the hole she's created. She follows us and we are all sucked through a tunnel and end up outside the underground city on the crest of a mountain looking down at the crumbling remains before our eyes.

"What happened?" Sarah asks.

"The Albion fleet is attacking our city. Mohryia was holding them back, but he has fled, abandoned us," Phesia says. "Here, you'll need these." She hands Ricky and I our wands.

"I told you," I say. "He has another agenda."

"Yes, that appears so," Phesia says. "All is lost. My people are dying." Looking at the carnage below, her eyes tear up.

"Have any escaped?" Ricky asks.

"Yes, a small group is headed into the valley of the serpents."

"Dragons' Run? They'll be killed," Sarah says.

"I cannot help them now."

"What do we do?" Ricky asks.

"We find a portal. I sensed one in Dragons' Run before," I say.

"Yes," Sarah agrees, "there is a strong force there, but it's surrounded by dragons."

"Yes, there is a time portal there, but to use it we'll have to use magic against them." Phesia says.

"Let's go then," I say. "I wonder what happened to Azandra's troops."

"They are chasing Mohryia, but he has gone into the past," Phesia says.

"They'll be able to find him," Ricky says. "Maybe, but he has learned many tricks about time travel and their sensors."

"Do you know them too?" Sarah asks.

"Of course, who do you think taught him?"

"But he has abandoned you and his people," I say. "So how can you still support him?"

"I don't, but that doesn't mean I agree with the Albions. I must find the survivors and help them, even if it means going into another time," Phesia says as we walk down the hillside into the valley of the dragons.

"Maybe we can help you," I say. Ricky and Sarah give me the evil eye. "Well, we obviously are not going to solve this by staying here and we don't agree with the destruction that the Albions or Mohryia have brought down on this world."

"Let's not get ahead of ourselves. We need to find my people first."

"Of course, Priestess, we just may be able to aid them in escaping this madness." As we slide past tops of trees, fire and shrieking rain down from above.

"Dragons! Quick, into the trees!" Phesia shouts. She waves her staff in the sky. "*Super Nos!*" The dragons cry and beat their wings but the fire only burns the trees and grass.

"A protection spell," Ricky says.

"*Protegit nos a draconibus!*" Phesia yells and her staff sends a blue shield around us so that none of the dragons' fire harm us.

"*Perdere!*" Ricky and I yell, aiming our wands at the beasts circling above. "*Perdere!*" The closest dragon is struck by our magic and falls to the ground. The other dragons fly away.

"Well done, young wizards," Phesia says as she keeps the shielding umbrella of force around us with her staff. "Now let's find my people before the dragons and raptors finish them off."

At the bottom of the valley as night falls, we can see fire in the distance. "That must be them," Sarah says.

"Hurry. They may be injured."

About half an hour later we're close enough to see their campfire and hear them talking.

"Outlanders! It is I, your priestess, Phesia!" The leader of these banished souls announces. Several of them grab weapons and aim them in our direction. "Look upon me," the priestess says, walking into their camp ahead of us.

"How could this be?" one of them asks. "The city is destroyed."

"The young wizards and I escaped harm and are here to rescue you." The eyes reflected in the firelight question us as we follow her in.

"They are with us then?" someone asks.

"Yes, Formorn, they have come to help us escape this mayhem," Phesia says.

"But, what of the Albion fleet? They will find us and kill us," Formorn says.

"Yes, they will track us," someone else says.

"Azandra and her fleet are after Mohryia. You don't need to worry about them, they are long gone through a time portal." After nervous introductions, we are given food to eat and bedding to rest on.

"What are we to do now, Priestess?" Formorn asks.

"With the wizards help we will leave this time for good and live our lives away from all of this hardship and death. Rest, and you will start a new journey tomorrow."

Ricky, Sarah and I lie down and rest for the first time in a long time. My thoughts are flooded with unknowns; *What has happened to Mohryia? Have Azandra's troops found him and eliminated his threat? How do the Dagon fit into all of this? And the Greys and Hybrids? Where will we take these people tomorrow? Our time? Some other time? What if the Albions track and follow us?*

I lie awake for a long time listening to the night. The owls and coyotes, not to mention the shrieks of the dragons and Fireraptors keep me awake. I hear Phesia renew her protection spell. The crackling fire comforts me as finally I drift off...

— CHAPTER SEVENTEEN —

The Future Past

"He has escaped through the portal, Commander," lieutenant Meyers says as their ship chases after Mohryia's.

"We're too late," Azandra says. "Find the portal, Bhinder."

"It has been cloaked by magic, Commander. I cannot get an accurate read on his position, nor can I find the portal he used," Bhinder replies.

"That is not good enough! We must not lose him."

"I will try to see through the veil, but it is very difficult. Magic changes the images and may not allow us to connect accurately."

"I don't care for your excuses. Find him! Meyers, have the seekers look for any evidence of residuals from his ship. Something is always left behind."

"Yes, Commander, I'm already on it. The tech officer says that he has found some residuals, but it is not absolute and the magic may have altered the co- ordinates of his entry into hyperspace."

"Even that is better than flying blind. Send those coordinates to the pilot."

"Immediately, sir."

Minutes later on the bridge, Azandra, her lieutenant and Meyers all wait for the pilot to lock in the coordinates.

"Locked in, Commander." He glances her way.

"Good. Engage."

The pilot moves a lever on the control panel and blue energy surrounds the ship, which wavers and then flashes forward into hyperspace. Space bends into a blur of color and stars all around them. After several minutes, they come to a halt. They find themselves back on Earth.

"What time or era are we at?" Azandra asks.

"We are back before the young wizards' time,

about 1900 or even earlier," Bhinder says. "I will know once we are out of the ship, and I can sense it more clearly."

"Meyers, you stay with the ship. Bhinder and you three," she points to three crew members on the bridge, "will go with me." Out of the ship, Azandra calls Meyers. "Cloak the ship but be ready to move if I need you."

"As you command." Immediately the ship disappears.

"I will call you when I have detected anything." She clicks the comm, and they head out. "Which way?"

"I feel a surge of energy to the west, Commander," Bhinder says.

About an hour later, they hear a humming noise over the next hill. "Be ready," Azandra orders, sliding her weapon in front of her. The others follow suit. As they reach the ridge, she waves them to a stop and looks through her scope. "There are at least four life forms ahead, but I cannot see Mohryia or a ship."

"He is not with them, Commander," Bhinder says. "He is in the tunnels below the ground. His ship is not visible. It must be cloaked."

"Yes, well, as long as he is not aware of us, we have a chance," Azandra says. "First, we take his soldiers, then we take him. Quickly and quietly, follow me." They narrow the gap between themselves and the Outlander soldiers until they are behind some rocks just meters away. "On my mark." Azandra waits until one of the enemy soldiers comes a little closer, then jumps out and stuns him before he can react. "Bhinder, stay with him." The four of them stalk the three Outlanders left and surprise two of them, but one is quick enough to get a shot back on them hitting one of Azandra's soldiers. She stuns him, but her comrade is killed.

They bring the other prisoners to Bhinder. "Watch these three," Azandra orders one of her soldiers who puts energy cuffs on them and stays while she and Bhinder head towards the tunnel.

"Is he still in the tunnel?" she asks her sentient. "Yes, but he is not moving. Also, I sense something else there. Intense energy."

"Is it the Crystal Codex?"

"Maybe, but it is a different energy surrounding the whole tunnel. We may be in danger if we enter."

"We don't have a choice. We must stop him before he enters our time and destroys New Albion." Azandra rushes forward into the tunnel. Unfortunately, the energy force is so strong that it freezes her in her tracks. Bhinder can do nothing except retreat and run back to the soldier on guard.

"We must leave for the ship at once!" she tells him. "But where is the commander?"

"Mohryia has her. We cannot help her now. Hurry!" They both hustle their prisoners back to the ship. "Lieutenant, get the ship ready!" The vessel appears in front of them and a hatch opens.

"Where is the commander? What happened?" Meyers asks.

"Mohryia has her and another weapon which threatens all of our lives. We must leave right now!" Bhinder says.

Meyers looks at them for a split second and turns to the pilot. "Get us into orbit immediately!" The pilot responds by levering the power control and sending them into orbit in seconds.

"What do we do now?" Bhinder asks.

"We wait, ready ourselves, and hopefully, save the commander," Meyers responds. "Activate the Crystal Codex!" His weapons officer pushes several buttons, and they are surrounded by blue energy. The ship vibrates with its power. "Focus on Mohryia's last coordinates."

"What about Azandra?" Bhinder says.

"Worse scenario, she's already dead. If not, we may be able to grab them both with the energy beam."

"What if he is using a crystal codex as well?" she asks.

"Then, we will have a standoff, I guess. At least we will have a chance."

At that moment, a great beam of energy flashes from the planet surface and disappears into the void. "Mohryia has re-entered the portal," Meyers says. "Follow them back to the future." The pilot sends them into the portal as well. They arrive back in the ice age, but there is no sign of Mohryia's ship. "Where did they go?"

"I do not know, Lieutenant, but they are not in this time. I cannot get a fix on them at all."

"Not again," Meyers says in frustration. "He can't just disappear. There must be some indication. Scan the residuals from here."

"I'm already trying, sir, but there is no sign of his ship," the tech officer says. "Hold on, the ship was here, but he did a double jump and is gone."

"Can you tell whether he went into the past or further into the future?" Meyers asks.

"No, sir."

"Bhinder, can you sense anything!"

"No, but let's be logical, it makes sense that he probably went back into the past as that is when the changes would occur to the time continuum, if that is his purpose."

"Why would he do that?" Meyers asks.

"By affecting certain factors, he can change the future of this reality so that the outcomes would be different. Not a total change of reality, just a tinkering."

"Just enough to do what?"

"Changing the creation of New Albion, perhaps?"

"That would make sense," Meyers says. "Especially if he wanted to rewrite his position in all of it."

"You mean, change his status and control?"

"Exactly, so we need to know when would be the best time for him to intervene."

"Would it make sense he would go back to before the disruptions of WW III?" Bhinder asks.

"Probably, all we can do is make a guess and hope we choose the right time. Pilot, set a course for 2020," Meyers orders. "Set in," the pilot answers after adjusting dials. "Engage," Meyers says, and they zip into hyperspace again.

— CHAPTER EIGHTEEN —

Azandra

"Where are we?" Formorn asks, looking around the beach surroundings.

"More important, when are we?" Phesia asks.

"Yes, well, both are important, actually," I say.

"We're in Australia before it was colonized. The year is 1756, about thirty years before the British penal colony so you don't have to worry about them. The only other people here are the aborigines and they've been here for millennia. Nobody, not even Mohryia should be able to find you. There is no ship to track when we use magic."

"So, we can start fresh with no worries of interference for some time?" Phesia asks.

"Exactly, and there should be enough fresh water to find, and food plants and animals to eat. Just don't interfere with the aborigines if you can help it and you should be alright until the British come in 1788 or so," I say.

"Brilliant," Sarah says, "I almost want to stay."

"We can't," Ricky speaks up, "if we want to stop Mohryia, we have to go back."

"Yes," I say. "Phesia, take good care of your people and enjoy your freedom."

"We will," she answers, "and thank you for your help. If not for you three, we would be lost."

"Maybe, we'll see you in the future," Ricky says.

"Or, maybe, in the past," Phesia says.

With that, Sarah, Ricky and I set our sights back on the future.

"What time should we go to?" Sarah asks.

"Our time, 2020. We need to go back to home base before we do anything else. By now, Mom will think we're lost or something."

"Thank goodness time is not the same in all timelines. She won't know how long we've actually been gone if we set the time correctly," Ricky says.

"When were we last there?" Sarah asks.

"Let me see." I try my best to think of the timeline.. "I don't remember what day of the week it was."

"I think it was a Tuesday," Sarah offers.

"Yes, that's right," Ricky says. "I had a quiz in chemistry which I bombed."

"Oh, well," I say, "You can rewrite it, can't you?"

"Yes, if we hurry and get there at the right time."

"We will, don't worry," I assure him.

"Ready?"

"Yup."

"Let's go."

We hold hands. I ready my wand. *"Futura praeturitis ad nos!"* I say while I keep the date in my head to aim for in 2020. The beach in Australia disappears and we fly through the time tunnel of colors and stars, landing in the middle of the intersection of Lampson Street and Esquimalt Road. Cars narrowly miss us as they honk their horns and swerve around us. We dash to the sidewalk.

"Whoa!" Sarah says, falling to the grass on someone's lawn. "What are you trying to do, Billy? Kill us? Next time, Ricky sets the spell!"

"Sorry. I don't know how that happened."

"Unless you misjudged the time by a few minutes because we were crossing the street at some point that day," Ricky says. "Remember? To get to the library."

"Right, but Sarah wasn't with us yet," I reasoned.

"I don't know. Something's changed then," Ricky says.

"Forget it for now," Sarah says. "I'm tired and hungry. Let's go home."

--*-*-*

"You're home a little late today," Mom says when we reach our front door.

"We had some research to do in the library," I say.

"Well, dinner is on the table."

"Thanks, Mom, I'm starving," Sarah says.

"Thanks for letting me be here so much," Ricky says.

"No, problem. You're like one of the family anyway."

"Well, I do appreciate it." Ricky's face gets a little flushed.

"I know you do." Mom gives him a hug. "Now let's eat it before it goes cold."

It felt good to be home again. All of this time travel stuff and end of the world talk had been getting to me and I was weary of it. Mohryia and his plans could wait for another day. We needed our regular lives back for a bit.

At school the next day, the three of us caught up with our studies and friends. Time-travel has changed us though, knowing we have to go back and face the uncertainty of the future. *Which reality do we really belong in?* Ricky agrees with me. Our perspective on time and reality have changed. As we walk home after school Sarah says she feels different too. It's hard for her to accept the immaturity of her friends; their thoughts seem to be so much about petty things—looks, clothes, favorite songs. It all seems so unimportant given what we now face. It would be easy for us just to stay in this reality. After all, it is our real lives, here and now, isn't it? But on the other hand, we have an obligation to the future, we said that we would help.

In class I'm distracted. I keep expecting Azandra to show up and demand we help her. I imagine her around every corner.

"I wonder what happened to her," Ricky says as we walk home on Thursday.

"We can't worry about it," I say. "Remember, time is different from ours. She might be still battling Mohryia."

"He may have killed her and obliterated New Albion too," he says.

"Yes, well, what could we have done?"

"We could have gone back right away."

"Anyway, it is what it is."

"True enough," he agrees, "Look, Sarah is coming."

I look around and see her jostling after us, so I stop and wait.

"Guys... guys... listen," she says, out of breath. "I...I...saw him."

"Saw who?" I ask.

"Mohryia. He was...on the school grounds."

"Are you sure it was him?" Ricky asks.

"Yup. Not too many people look like him."

"Did he see you?" I ask.

"No, I don't think so. I ducked behind the wall and when I peeked out, he wasn't there."

"Let's get home before he finds us."

When we reach Greenwood Avenue, a dark cloud is circling ahead of us. Sparks fly as it moves towards us.

"What's that?" Sarah asks as we walk down the hill.

"I don't know, sis, but we better get out of its way." We run under some oak trees nearby. We watch from the safety of their boughs as the wind picks up and the cloud circles above, the air crackling around us.

"*Protegat* nos!" I yell, using my wand to surround us in a protection spell.

A figure flashes from the cloud, a wand in his hand. "*Duratus!*" A blue flash erupts from his wand. The light identifies him.

"*Duratus!*" Mohryia hollers as he advances through the air and lands beside us.

"*Mohryia, et abierunt!*" Ricky yells, his wand sending a blue beam at the unwelcome wizard. He remains, deflecting the spell with his wand.

"*Inrita magicae!*" he shouts.

"*Duratus!*" I yell.

Mohryia laughs. "You will not use magic on me."

"Why have you followed us?" Sarah asks.

"Yes, you have what you want. We're not fighting you," Ricky says.

"True, but your presence is requested in the future. Now, come quietly or I will have to force you."

103

"Not if we can stop you!" I yell, pointing my wand at him. "*Mohryia et abierunt!*"

Mohryia laughs harder. "Your magic will not work. I have blocked you. Now come peacefully and I will not harm you."

"Come on, guys, we don't have a choice."

"*Et ascendere me,*" Mohryia says and we're lifted up beside him and rise into his ship.

"What's happened to Azandra?" Sarah asks as we are escorted to locked seats.

"She is alive. And you can see for yourself soon. Now relax and we will be there before you know it." "Humph." Sarah scrunches up her face as Mohryia smiles and leaves the room. The ship jolts forward and we're traveling through time again. After several seconds, we slow to a stop. Mohryia re-enters the room and releases us.

"Is New Albion still there?" I ask, fearing the worst.

"Of course it is," he answers, his smile like a Cheshire cat's. "Not quite the same but you'll recognize it. Open it," he directs the pilot, who pushes a button on the control panel and the hatch to the orb surrounding the city opens allowing us entry. When we arrive atop the landing platform, I notice a greeting committee. Several councilors are there, but not Rhunella or Azandra or Rodan. Also, I see a group of Outlander soldiers in a column behind them.

"Welcome, Your Excellency," says one of the councilors, bowing as he walks forward. I frown at the salute. *When did Mohryia become Your Excellency?*

"Is all in order, Rahgyar?" Mohryia addresses him, his hand raised.

"Yes, yes, all is in order, sir," the bowing servant says. "Shall I prepare the feast for you?"

"Yes, get on with it." Mohryia waves him away. He turns to another councilor. "Have you contacted Rodan, Friedlund?"

"Ah." A smallish, balding man in a grey outfit moves forward. "No, sire, but we are searching all of the usual contacts."

"Not good enough, Friedlund!" Our captor aims a finger at the shaking little man. "I want him found before he gets what he needs. Our lives depend upon it!"

"Yes, yes, your grace, I am on it," Friedlund answers and scurries away. Mohryia lowers his hand and turns to us.

"Now then, you must be famished. Councilors, ready the great chamber for our meal," he says, clapping his hands and shooing the rest of the greeting party away. "We have much to discuss."

In the great chamber, one lone figure sits at the big table. "Azandra," Ricky and I cry out as we rush to her. Her eyes are glazed over, looking aimlessly through us. "Are you okay?" I ask. No answer. Her lifeless eyes have lost some of their purple as she continues to stare straight ahead, motionless.

"What have you done to her?" Sarah reaches out and lifts her limp, grey hand. "She's cold!"

"Yes," Mohryia answers. "She's lost some of her...aggressiveness. She's much more agreeable now."

"Agreeable?" I argue. "She's a robot. What of Rhunella and the other councilors?"

"Unfortunately, they all left before I came. I don't know what happened to them."

"And why are you after Rodan?" I ask.

"He thinks he is going to save the city, but alas, as you can see, it's too late for that."

"What about the people?" Sarah asks.

"Well, under new management they have become quite docile. The war is over and we can live in peace now. That's what everybody wanted, after all."

"Yes, but you've turned them into morons," Ricky shouts at him.

"They have chosen their path. You are either with me or you will be."

"What does that mean?" Sarah asks.

"You have a choice. You can join me or, if you choose not to, I can convince you to join me."

"Really?" I say. "And how are you going to do that?"

He sighs and grins. "You must be tired. Why don't you rest and we can revisit it in the morning? Rahgyar, show them to their quarters."

"This way," the servant says, waving us forward. He presses an exterior panel to the room we entered, and a force field blocks us from leaving.

"What are we going to do?" Sarah asks, plopping into a chair.

"Well, for starters, we're not going to agree with him," I say.

"Yeah, we'll figure something out," Ricky says. "There's always a way."

CHAPTER NINETEEN

Rodan

"But, Tolov, Mohryia is threatening to use the Crystal Codex to destroy us," Regent Rodan argues. "Next, he'll be attacking your race."

"We are not worried about a minor wizard," Tolov answers. "We have other ways of dealing with wayward magicians."

"That's just it. We need your help! Do I need to beg?"

"Of course not. It's just that your coalition attacked first, when you destroyed the Outlander city." "That was not the coalition. Azandra acted independently and without agreement from the Council."

"Still, it happened and hundreds of lives were lost. If it weren't for the three young wizards all of the Outlanders would be dead now."

"Yes, they helped some to escape, but I believe Mohryia has captured them again."

"It would be a shame for them to suffer because of your mistakes, true. Let me look in the Eye of Destiny," Tolov says as he manipulates dials and buttons on a control panel which projects various scenes on the chamber wall. "Here we go. They seem to be held within a force field in a room in New Albion. They are not harmed."

"Can you help them?" the regent asks.

"Of course, this moment was meant to happen, but as far as the coalition is concerned, you have a long way to go before I will change your reality. It is yours to fix."

"So, you won't help us fight Mohryia? He will come after your race next."

"Of course he will, and we will be ready for him. All of these things are foreseen."

"Not if he has changed part of the future. The Crystal Codex was designed for that purpose."

"Yes, and all of the options are anticipated in the program."

"But how do you know which option he has set in motion?"

"There are certain indicators which allow us to predict what will happen."

"With one hundred percent accuracy?"

"Not quite, more like ninety-five percent depending on unforeseen variables."

"Such as?"

"Time, numbers of participants, freedom of choice...etc..."

"That sounds more like guesswork."

"Well, life is guesswork, but we can put in the equalization equation which will show what out- comes are more likely."

"You are banking on more likely? That does not sound very scientific for your race."

"Even science has to include unknowns, Rodan. You must know that, given the precariousness of the lunar outposts, Martian cities and floating cities in between. How many failures did you encounter before you succeeded?"

"Yes, well, we had all variables accounted for by the end of the first settlement's review, less than six months. Bottom line, are you going to deal with this or not?"

"We already are. Your wizards will be free of their confinement momentarily. Here, you can watch." Tolov switches several panel controls and the picture of the wizards' room in New Albion shows the force field disappearing.

"But, what of Mohryia?"

"The wizards are not just free. They have been given back their ability to do magic as well. There is a ninety-seven point five percent chance of a favorable outcome for them in escaping completely or finding a way to stop Mohryia."

"What? How? You're beginning to sound like a lab experiment."

"Life is an experiment and it's been going on here since the planet first showed signs of life. Your species has modified the human mammals for centuries and now you have hybrids, just like on your Martian colony millennia ago."

"Yes, and your species has modified reptilian forms as well. Look at the Venusian colony."

"All advanced species with intelligence end up changing DNA of their own and other life forms. It is a natural result of progressing civilizations."

"Yes, of course, but you're willing to let this dangerous situation resolve itself ? What if Mohryia destroys New Albion in the process?"

"I'm willing to step in if absolutely necessary, but the young wizards have shown amazing ability to overcome obstacles. We need to let them try first."

"You play a dangerous game, Tolov. You could be wrong and then our world would be destroyed!"

"That is why I am going to allow you to carry the intervention with you, but you will not be able to activate it without my final agreement."

"But, how do I know you approve?"

"Don't worry, I'll be watching it from here; all you'll need to do is ask for my permission."

"Okay then, as you insist, just let me have the intervention device now so we have a chance to enact it if necessary."

"Of course." Tolov reaches for a small tube in a compartment in the panel. "To start the sequence merely turn the device in your hands." He demonstrates a twisting motion with his hands as he gives it to Rodan.

Rodan pockets the tube in his cape. "Thank you. I must leave immediately." He shakes Tolov's hand, turns and leaves the room. "To New Albion with all haste!" he says to the pilot of his ship, who activates the antigrav drive and they ascend out of the sea.

--*-*-*

"Billy, what happened?" Sarah says, noticing the hum of the force field has stopped.

"I think the force field is down," her brother says. "Wait a second." He takes one shoe off and pitches it at the doorway and it sails through without incident.

"We're good then?" Sarah asks.

"Yup," Ricky answers as he walks out of the room.

"What now?" Sarah nervously looks around as they walk down the hallway.

"Do we have our magic back?" Ricky asks.

"Good question, let's check." I raise my wand. *"Fac mihi interitum."*

"Good. Hold my hand," Ricky says, reaching for Sarah's hand. *"Ut maneant nobiscum."* They both disappear as well.

"Let's hope that Mohryia doesn't notice us," I say as we walk toward the observation room where the Central Control Agency of New Albion used to be. As we approach the entrance, I notice that it looks the same except that the soldiers are Outlanders not Albions. Mohryia is watching the screens intently.

"Well, young ones, you are more resourceful than I thought. I don't know how you dispensed with the force field, but it will do you no good. I am too powerful for you," he says, almost ignoring us.

"In frigore milites," I say. The Outlander soldiers freeze in their places.

"In frigore et arioles," Mohryia shouts and Ricky and I freeze, but he doesn't account for Sarah who is still able to move. She grabs a hand weapon from one of the soldiers and blasts Mohryia who falls back onto the floor. *"In me transierunt,"* he yells and disappears.

If I can just get my wand to activate. *"Regello,"* I say and Ricky and I regain control over our bodies.

"Nos visibili," Ricky says and we all suddenly ap pear.

"Good thinking, sis."

"Should we follow him?" Ricky asks.

"No, I think we should secure New Albion first."

"Look," Sarah says, "What's that on the screen?" We watch as a ship blasts several Outlander soldiers on the landing deck and proceeds to land. New Albion soldiers descend to the platform.

"It's Rodan with part of the fleet," Ricky says. "They're entering the city."

After a short time, Rodan is rushing down the corridor towards us.

"Ah, young wizards, you are okay," he says, entering the CCA. "I feared that Mohryia would have killed you already, but Tolov has more faith in you and assured me you would find a way to challenge him. Where is he?"

"He has escaped to the past," Sarah says.

"Do you know when?" Rodan asks.

"No, but there are several options—1891, 2020 or 1778."

"Which one makes the most sense?" Rodan asks.

"Let's see, if it's 1778, he's discovered where the Outlander survivors are."

"I doubt that," Ricky says.

"Okay, 1891 would mean he is after something magical or powerful."

"What do you mean?" Rodan asks.

"Magical would be something related to the Dragon and Chinese magic," I say.

"And powerful would have something to do with the Crystal Codex," Sarah says.

"Exactly, so my guess is he's in that time," Ricky says.

"Why not 2020?"

"That's our real time, so if he knows we're here, why would he go there?" I answer.

"Okay then, let's go after him with my ship and troops. My men have secured the city, so we'll take part of the fleet with us and defeat him once and for all."

"Sarah, you stay here where you're safe," I say. "No, I'm as much a part of this as you two are."

She waves her hand weapon around. "Careful with that," Rodan says.

"I know how it works. I already used it on Mohryia."

Rodan raises his eyebrows. "Really? I guess I've underestimated you."

"Alright, sis, but follow my lead, okay?"

"Of course, big brother, but if you get into trou ble, I'll save you." She smiles. I laugh and smile back.

Dragon Fire

"Take us to eighteen ninety-one," Rodan tells the pilot on the bridge.

"Plotted and set, sir," the pilot answers as he moves dials and presses buttons. We feel the ship wa- ver and we exit into the ether.

"Can you sense him?" I ask Sarah when we're on the ground, outside of the ship.

"Yes," she answers, "but I can't tell you where yet."

"This looks a lot like the area we were in before," Ricky says. "When we found the Chinese railroad workers by that mine."

"What's he talking about?" Rodan queries as his troops stand ready behind him.

"When we first noticed Mohryia, it was in this time," I answer.

"Well then, which way should we search?"

"Sarah?" I ask.

"Let's start by going over by those trees," she replies, pointing at the forest in front of us.

"Okay," I say leading us. As we got near the trees I notice a path between two big firs. "Let's follow this path." The fresh breeze and the smell of thick firs reminds me of my walks in Saxe Point Park back home. I feel energized and alert. Birds and insects buzz around our heads. About an hour in we come across an open space with a fire pit in the middle. The coals are smoking slightly, which tells me that someone was there not long ago.

"Be ready, men," Rodan orders. "Mohryia could be anywhere ahead. Wizards, let me and my men go first to give you a warning, so your magic is more likely to have a chance of success."

I stop and nod. Rodan leads his men forward. We follow with Sarah between Ricky and myself. As we reach the top of a hill, the sun's fading rays strike us. At least it's warmer than the ice age. Looking down, we see a river running through a lush, green vale.

"I sense Mohryia in the valley below," Sarah says.

"Rodan!" I call and wait for him to respond.

"Yes?" He stops his men, turning to face me.

"Sarah senses Mohryia below."

"Good. Shirem, take a few men and scout their position." Shirem nods his head and taps two soldiers near him. They trot down the path. "Wizards, we will camp here for the night and await the scouts' return. Low fires, men, and rations. Porter, you, and Harley will be first watch, one up and one down of our camp. Use your comm if you see anything."

"Yes, Commander," they respond and head off to their posts.

--*-*-*

"A dragon is attacking us!" Ricky yells at me and I jump up from my sleep.

"*Congelo est Draco!*" I scream, sending a blue bolt from my wand and the dragon pauses, but doesn't stop. *Why isn't the magic working?* "Ricky, with me."

"*Congelo est Draco!*" we yell together. The beast pauses again, but doesn't stop. It circles and rises, wings spread and beating furiously.

"*Et ignis hostes eorum, Draco!*" Someone yells. I look behind the dragon and see Mohryia, wand out, eyes sparkling with red fire. "Now, you will be finished!" he says. The dragon dives toward us, fire roaring from its gaping mouth, claws bared, ready to fry us and tear us apart.

"Ricky, we must stop it!" I scream.

"Stop what?" a voice breaks through my consciousness and I awake with a start, sweat dripping from my every pore.

"Oh my God, Billy, are you alright?" Sarah asks, unzipping her sleep bag and reaching for me.

"Yes, ah...I guess so," I stammer as she hugs me. "I must have been dreaming." Wiping my brow after she lets go of me, I'm embarrassed and horrified by my dream. "Good thing it was only a dream; we were about to be toasted by dragon fire."

"All is quiet right now, Billy," Ricky says. "No dragons, no fire, no Mohryia anywhere."

"Rodan." He comes over to us. "Have the scouts returned?"

"No. I've sent two more to find out what happened to them."

"Have they returned?"

"No. I was about to wake you—"

"Billy!" Sarah shouts. "Mohryia is coming!" A cold wind blows up the mountain onto us, almost knocking us off our feet.

"What the heck was that?" Ricky says.

We hear an intense growl and suddenly a winged creature sprays fire at us.

"*Protegit nos a Draconibus!*" I spread a protection spell around us, and the dragon fire washes over without burning us.

"*Ne Draconum!*" Ricky shouts, sending blue bolts. The dragon pauses, bats its wings and vomits more fire at us.

"*Protegit!*" But the dragon doesn't stop. It rears back and rises high over the trees as if called by someone. Then, we see Mohryia alighting on its back, wand in hand, cape flowing behind. We watch as the evil wizard charges down at us. The dragon shrieks as it brings him closer and closer.

"Billy, do something," Sarah says as the soldiers aim their weapons at the beast.

"Fire!" Rodan shouts. The soldiers send volleys of blue energy skyward.

"*Protegit!*" Mohryia yells protecting himself and the dragon. The blue energy beams deflect away from our attacker. "*In frigore milites!*" A green blast from his wand freezes all of the soldiers including Rodan.

"*In frigore et ariolos!*" Mohryia shouts and Ricky and I are frozen on the spot. Sarah fires her weapon at him but it deflects. The dragon and Mohryia land with a thud in front of us. "*Duratus puella!*" he says, and Sarah freezes in mid-firing of her gun. "*Veni mecum!*" Sarah is lifted and lands behind Mohryia on the dragon's back. "Goodbye, young wizards. Hopefully, you will see that fighting me is useless and join my new future."

"*Dimittere eos!*" Mohryia, the dragon, and Sarah fly away in a flash as the feeling returns to our bodies.

"He has Sarah," Ricky wails.

"What now, Wizards?" Rodan says. "I have a weapon that can stop him which Tolov gave me, but I cannot use it without his agreement."

"Okay, but he has Sarah so we'll have to be careful or he'll harm her," I say. The soldiers wake up, scratching their heads and looking confused.

"Tolov," Rodan says. "I need your approval."

CHAPTER TWENTY-ONE

Sarah

"*Regello!*" Mohryia says, freeing Sarah from his spell.

"Wh..where are you taking me?" she asks, clinging onto his cape, the wind whipping in her face as she tries to see where the dragon is taking them.

"Don't worry," he answers, "you will be safe. I have a special place that I want you to see." Sarah shivers as she hangs on for dear life, watching the land fly by as they dip and swirl on the back of the foul beast that smells like sulphur.

"*Aperiesque ostium!*" Mohryia shouts as he trains his wand in front of the dragon that rears his huge head and halts in mid-air. A beam of green light flashes from his wand, pointing in the distance where a swirling green circle expands out of thin air. "Fly into the circle, Menhora!" the wizard yells. The dragon snaps forward, entering the circle. The stars behind them disappear as they're drawn through at frightening speed. Sarah feels static charges all over her body. Before she knows where they are the dark sky above with the stars reappears, but the cold air has gone, warmth now embracing her.

After about half an hour of shaking, the flying serpent slows down, circles a mountain peak, then descends to a walled fortress with fiery towers and weird noises as if they're coming from howling scepters. Sarah, gaze frozen on the spectacle below, holds her breath in terrible fascination. Winged creatures cackle and shriek like a welcoming chorus of evil as Mohryia descends.

"What are they?" Sarah says, her heart pounding, limbs aching from the strain of holding on.

"My pets, my dear," Mohryia says. "Aren't they beautiful?"

"Not the word I was thinking of," she answers. "Where did they come from?"

"I created them, of course. Menhora, set us down gently. We have precious cargo." The dragon bats its huge wings backwards to ease our descent, alighting in the middle of the strange arena of creatures that howl with delight.

"Quiet, quiet, my lovelies. I've brought you a new friend." The beasts settle down and fold their wings in silence. Menhora lowers her great girth so that Sarah can easily step onto the ground. She chokes and coughs from the stench of the stinking beasts. The creatures lean in close.

"Back, back!" Mohryia commands. "Give her room!"
Sarah stares at the unholy menagerie of dragon-kind and other strange animals. Some with long, split tongues between razor sharp jaws, others with long claws and boney snouts or horns on their heads.

They back up and sniff the air getting a whiff of her scent.
"You like her?" Mohryia asks, smiling at Sarah. Some of them nod their heads, but one snarls at her, saying, "Delicious."

"Yuck!" Sarah says. "Why would you make beasts like these? Why not deer, antelope, fuzzy cats, or dogs even?"

"We are no longer on your planet. The animals here are quite different. I decided to help by creating some new animals for us and I'm especially fond of dragons, griffins, raptors and the like. They're not only special, but they're also much more useful in a fight."

"Okay..." Sarah says, "but did you have to make them talk, too?"

"They won't know what to do if they don't understand me, will they?"

"I guess, but it just seems kind of cruel."

"They don't mind, my dear. Now, how about a good meal? You must be hungry."

Sarah looks around at her predicament. The creatures coo and grumble around her; some smiling while others lick their lips and laugh. "Welcome," a griffin-like creature says.

"I guess I don't have much choice." She frowns and follows Mohryia as he directs her towards a door in the inner sanctum. She feels relief as she steps inside the huge, warm room with a great fireplace belching out heat. Light flickers from the wall torch- es. A large wooden table sits in the middle with chandeliers hanging over it. Mohryia walks over and pulls one of the big wooden chairs out.

"Sit down," he says as he waves his hand and speaks a spell, "*Mensamque.*" The table loads itself up with a tablecloth, plates, cutlery, mugs, lit candles, serviettes, salt and pepper. "Timmons!" he calls, and a horned manlike creature rushes out from the hallway in the back.

"Yes, sire?"

"Bring the meat and vegetables right away."

"Of course, sire." Timmons spins on his heels and departs to the back. Sarah carefully slides into the seat that is readied for her, watching as several half-person, half-beast servants enter the dining room with trays of meat, vegetables, sauces, gravy, pickles and condiments of all kinds. Finally, a teapot full of tea is brought.

A servant lady with three eyes, scaly skin, and a tail, says, "I hope you like peppermint, miss." She pours the hot liquid into a cup, then sets it down on the table.

"Yes, thank you," Sarah answers. "Would you try some first, Mohryia?"

"Of course, my dear. I assure you it is only tea." He takes a sip from his own cup, swallows, smiling at her. Sarah's stomach growls as she smells roast beef, mashed potatoes, steaming vegetables and gravy. "You are hungry. Have a good meal first, then we will talk further." Without answering, Sarah fills her plate with the delicious food. Mohryia does the same, and after some time they converse further.

"What about my brother and Ricky? What do you have in mind for them?"

"They are welcome to join my new Albion as well," Mohryia says as he finishes his tea. "No harm will come to them if they agree to my terms. In fact, I am willing to make them equals and teach them all of my secrets about wizardry, spells, incantations and all."

"And what of the other humans? And Aliens?"

119

"All will live in peace if they agree to my arrangements, my rules, my small requirements."

"What makes you think that they will agree with your terms?"

"It is easy. I have the ability to reduce their world to rubble if they don't."

"But it is your world too."

"True, and I promise a peaceful existence."

"Yes, but you would control it. Just the arrangement that you and the Outlanders rebelled against."

"Perhaps, but with the young wizards' help we could ensure a safe, peaceful planet."

"So, your saying that if Billy and Ricky agree to help you run your new kingdom, no harm will come to anyone? What about the Dagon? Does Tolov agree with you?"

"Not yet, but he hasn't disagreed either. If your brother and friend join me, I'm sure he will know it is the only way to resolve this war once and for all."

"So, what does my being here have to do with all this? I'm not a witch or wizard."

"No, but you have abilities which make you important to the future. You are a seer and your ability to seek beings as they travel in time is important. Also, you are a sensitive."

"What does that mean?"

"You sense future events and can support their proper resolution by communicating to us wizards. You could help me save lives instead of letting them be killed."

"I might also help you eliminate people who are against your policies or rulings."

"I assure you that would never be my intention. You must see that I trust your abilities by bringing you here instead of just killing you? What a waste that would be."

"Not to mention horrific for me, my brother and Ricky." Sarah's face heats with fear. "Are you telling me that if I don't agree with you, I will be eliminated?"

"Of course not. You have an opinion and I respect that, but surely you see the futility of contradicting the logic of my statements."

"What are you expecting from me?"

"Well, you are tired. It has been a long harrowing day for you. Let me have my servant show you to your guest room and you can sleep on it. We'll talk in the morning. Timmons!" Almost instantly the horned servant rushes to our table from the back hall.

"Yes, sire?" he answers, the bobble hanging from his horns swinging around in front of his face. The wrap he wears around his middle, his horns, and hooved feet make him look like the Minotaur from Greek mythology.

"Take our guest to her room so she can freshen up and have a good rest."

"As you wish, sire," Timmons says, bows, and waves his arm in the direction of the staircase, bidding Sarah to follow him. She pushes her chair back and faces Mohryia. "Good night."

"Good night, my dear."

"Oh, thank you for dinner," Sarah says as she heads for the stairs to follow Timmons.

"You're welcome," the wizard says, his smile a little too wide.

— CHAPTER TWENTY-TWO —

New Albion

"Aren't we going to rescue Sarah?" I ask as Rodan has the pilot set a course for New Albion.

"I have to confer with Azandra and Rhunella first."

"I thought she was under Mohryia's control and Rhunella is not there," Ricky complains.

"Actually, Rhunella and Azandra are being held under special guard there. I'm hoping we can free them with our forces. The rest of the fleet is joining us for an attack on the domed city. Our scouts tell us that Mohryia is not there."

"But, what about Sarah?" I ask. "Do you know where she is?"

"The sentients tell me she is in another realm with Mohryia."

"What?" Ricky asks.

"Where?" I say.

"The Hybrids tell us they have gone through a vortex to a parallel universe, essentially, another Earth."

"And can we get there?" I ask.

"Yes, if the sentients can locate the vortex. In the meantime, we need to rescue Rhunella and Azandra and take back New Albion."

"As long as we go after Sarah as soon as the vortex is found," I add.

"Of course," Rodan says. "Don't worry. We will get her back and stop Mohryia at the same time."

As the domed city comes into view, I feel an urgency in regaining the city. Several of the New Albion fleet ships are orbiting as we approach the por- tal window which is closed.

"How do we enter?" Ricky asks.

"Can you use your magic to fool the guards?" Rodan asks.

"Maybe I can disguise myself as Mohryia," I answer, taking out my wand. "Let me try. *Ut me Mohryia.*" I feel a slight change in height and body as I transform into our nemesis.

"Excellent," Rodan says.

"Whoa, that's pretty good," Ricky says.

I smile and step towards the comm visual. "Open the portal!" I command as the disguised wizard.

A confused guard in the visual says, "I thought you were out of contact, sire?"

"Plans have changed. Open the portal!"

"Yes, sire. As you command." We watch as the hatch opens to allow us entry to New Albion.

"I have one of the wizards with me and several soldiers who have joined our cause," I say.

"We will meet you on the landing, sire. Anything else you require?"

"Yes, bring the prisoners to the great room at once. I need to talk with them."

"Immediately, your highness."

"And much of the Albion fleet will be landing as well, all joining our forces."

"Very good news, sire. Our men will escort them to the chamber."

"We will see you in the great room, soldier," I say and close the comm visual.

On the landing platform, we are greeted by several soldiers.

As the rest of Rodan's fleet land we follow Mohryia's soldiers to the great room. I see Azandra and Rhunella seated at the big table facing us. When the doors are closed Rodan directs his soldiers to stay back against the walls. This leaves the fooled forces in between. At my signal, Ricky and I face them.

"*Duratus!*" We both say waving our wands toward them. Blue energy surrounds them all and they freeze where they stand.

"Good!" Rodan says, then rushes to Azandra and Rhunella, but the two women remain unresponsive. "They're under some kind of spell. Can you help them?"

"We'll try," I answer. "*Regello eos!*" The energy from my spell strikes them, but they remain under whatever spell has captured them. "Together, Ricky." "*Regello eos!*" We shout together. This time the two councilors slowly thaw as if energy is melting from their bodies, the green energy dissipating from them into the air. They both slump forward onto the table,

"Azandra! Rhunella!" Both draw breaths and sit up. The color comes back to their faces. Azandra looks at us, bats her purple eyes and shakes her head. "Have I been asleep?" she questions as Rhunella moans, sits up and rubs her eyes. "What happened?" she says.

"Mohryia put you under a spell, but the young wizards have rescued you," Rodan explains.

"Where is he?" Rhunella looks around for him. "I remember he had attacked the city and we were captured."

"He's no longer with us," I say. "He's taken Sarah hostage and gone to another realm."

"Oh, no," Azandra says. "Obviously, he's planning some kind of attack, but what?"

"If he's gone to some other planet, there must be something there he can use against us," Rhunella reasons.

"Some of the portals go to specific galaxies," Rodan says.

"We need to find the portal he used," I say. "We can't follow him without knowing where to go and rescue Sarah."

"Why her?" Ricky asks.

"She has abilities like the sentients. She can locate people through time and she can foretell events," I say.

"Soldiers! Secure the city!" Rodan commands. The fleet of warriors departs the room. He picks up his comm. "Bhinder!"

"Yes, Commander."

"Have you located the portal yet?"

"Yes, it is 36 degrees north and 124 degrees east of your present position."

"Good. I will join you on the ship presently. Have the pilot set our heading."

"Yes, sir."

"Yokam!" Rodan calls on the comm.

"Commander?"

"Outfit your ship and call Nortsom to set these coordinates...36 degrees north...124 degrees east. We will be leaving as soon as possible."

"Yes, Commander."

"Rodan, we need to leave now!" I say, thinking about my sister.

"Of course. Azandra, are you well enough to join us?"

"Yes!" she answers, her eyes brightening with new purpose.

"Rhunella, will you take charge of New Albion and the prisoners?"

"I'm already on it, Rodan. You and the wizards rescue the girl, and if you are successful in stopping Mohryia, bring him to me. He has a lot to answer for." She wraps her shawl around her head and sets off to put New Albion back in order. "Rodan, leave most of the fleet here to guard the city and report back as soon as you can."

"Certainly," he says. "It is good to see both of you well and back to normal."

"Let's go!" Azandra says, leading us out of the room.

— CHAPTER TWENTY-THREE—

Zeldor

In the morning, Sarah awakens to the sound of birds outside her window. Looking out over the courtyard, the warm sun feels good on her face. She eyes a flock of beautiful multi-colored birds about the size of crows, but much prettier, swooping and diving in and out of the small trees. Their red and blue feathers contrast against the colorful yellow bushes and green grass below. Some of the creatures she saw the night before are stretching, yawning and stomping about the grassy foliage. They don't seem quite as scary standing several meters below in the sunshine. Beyond the walls of the fortress, Sarah takes in the green meadows, trees and majestic, purple mountains rising in the distance, their tops shrouded in wispy clouds.

"What a beautiful place," she whispers to herself. "I wonder if other beings live here, and does Mohryia control them too?" She can make out a herd of some kind running over the fields, but they're too far away to distinguish what animals they are. They are grazing and drinking water from a meandering river that cuts through the meadow as it spills out from the forest. A warm breeze enters through the open window. She leans forward to breathe in more of the fresh air. A sweet smell similar to lavender surprises her. Maybe this world offers more than just harsh wizards and scary animals. Hearing voices, she leans forward to see servants doing morning chores; feeding horse-like creatures, gathering eggs, milking cow-like beasts, taking vegetables from a garden. The horse beasts have manes like what she's used to, but their heads are more like dogs with horns like a deer.

After a while a large bird catches her attention as it flies from the forest beyond the meadow. As it nears, she can see it's not a bird at all, but a dragon with a caped rider carrying a staff. On the end of it a red stone glints in the sunshine.

Another wizard? I wonder if he's here on Mohryia's request or to challenge him. As the sorcerer flies over the castle wall Sarah eyes him carefully. *He's a wizard alright; ordinary soldiers don't carry scepters and fly on dragons.* The courtyard creatures scatter and squawk as he descends slowly.

"Rentwrath, stop growling. You can't still be upset over the trip. You have many friends here," the wizard, with long blond hair, moustache, and green eyes, scolds his steed. He jumps off the dragon, flips in the air and lands on his boots. The dragon grumbles something incoherent, swishes its tail at the barnyard animals as it saunters over to the water trough, dips its great head and slurps up half of the water in it.

"Ah! That's better." Rentworth snarls, burps, and smiles up at Sarah.

The wizard laughs, looks up to her bedroom, saying, "That was uncalled for. Don't scare Mohryia's guest."

"Pardon," the dragon says as he sarcastically bows to her. Sarah doesn't know whether she should laugh or cry, so she does neither.

"He means no harm, miss. He's rude by nature."

"And who are you?" she asks, opening the window a little wider.

"Shardee, at your service." The sorcerer half- bows.

"Hello. I'm Sarah. Pleased to meet you, I think." She hesitates for a moment then continues. "Where am I?"

"You are on Zeldor, of course," the dragon says. "Where else would you be?"

"Now, Rentworth, don't be rude. Perhaps she is from another realm."

"Indeed, I'm from Earth."

"Yes," Shardee says, "that's where Mohryia hails from. Ah, here he is now. Hello, good sage, I see you've brought a friend from Earth. How delightful."

"Yes, good to see you, Shardee. Keeping the locals in line I hope?"

"Yes, well, we had a little skirmish by Ravenwood, but I think my forces have cleaned that up."

"Good, good. Come in and we'll talk over a good breakfast. You must be famished. Forked Mountain is some ways from here." Sarah watches as the two wizards climb the castle stairs. She turns away from the window, snatches up a brush on the dresser and removes the knots out of her long, brown hair.

I wonder where the boys are. They won't know where I am, if they're not captured by Mohryia's troops by now.

A heavy knock on the door shifts her attention. She opens the door to Timmins telling her it's time for breakfast.

"I'll be right out," she says through the crack.

"Okay," the servant answers and waits there. She closes the door, gets dressed, and leaves the room. She follows him down the hall to the stairs where she can see many guests sitting around the great table. Most appear to be wizards with capes, special rings, beards and moustaches, except for two very beautiful women dressed in long bejeweled dresses and tiaras in their hair. All have green eyes, except the dark-haired woman who has purple eyes. I wonder if she's from Earth.

"Ah, here she is. Miss Sarah, I trust you slept well?" Mohryia asks.

"Well enough," Sarah answers curtly.

"She's feisty, I like that," Shardee says. Most of the gentlemen laugh.

"Are you a witch, my dear?" the blond-haired lady asks.

"Not exactly," Sarah says, "but I do have abilities."

"And what would they be?" the woman presses.

"I see into the future, for one, and what do you do?"

"Oh, I have many tricks, my dear," she answers with a grin.

"I can turn people into toads or bats or any other unnatural thing I choose, for one."

"Lovely," Sarah mutters.

"What was that?" the dark- haired witch asks.

"Ah, nothing," Sarah answers.

"Perhaps we should introduce ourselves," Mohryia says, deflecting the conversation. "You all know me, so let's start to my right and work around the table."

"Yes, well, I am Belinda of Weaverstown," the blond-haired witch says.

"And I am Dracous of Gravesward," an elderly balding gentleman with a white beard and purple cape says next.

"Tartarus from Dragonside," a tall, dark man with black hair and moustache in a scarlet cape says.

"I'm Shardee of Ravenwood," says the handsome blond wizard.

"I'm Sarah from Earth, but you already know as much." She frowns.

"Preshad of Morningside." A handsome, blue- haired mage with blue beard to match and a black cape.

"Leylandria of Moorshfelt." The dark-haired witch flashes her jeweled rings and bangles on her wrists.

"Mazore from Griffinland," a tall, black-haired mage with full beard says, wiping his hairy face and causing a green jewel in his beard to sparkle. His green cape makes him look like a Christmas ornament.

"And, I'm Daughtry of Coldspar," a small greying wizard says, flicking his ringed fingers at Sarah, shifting his blue cape around him.

"Well then, thank you all for coming at my request. As I've already told you, events on my home planet have deteriorated to the point where we could lose the battle against the Greys, the Hybrids and the Dagons. I hold New Albion, but barely. The City of Light has collapsed and the New Albion fleet is reorganizing to counterattack. If I don't return with allies soon, all could be lost."

"Why should we get involved with your problems on your planet?" Daughtry asks.

"Yes," Leylandria concurs. "Why, indeed? They could come here and threaten our existence."

"Only the wizards and some of the aliens have that ability," Mohryia argues. "There isn't much chance of that. Besides, I have the Crystal Codex."

"What's to stop them from using it against us?" Shardee joins the conversation.

"Well, to begin with, only the Dagon have that capability and they are not against my fight. I have already used it in New Albion with immediate success. I don't think they will chance my using it again."

"What do you suggest should be our extent of involvement?" Shardee asks.

"Yes, and furthermore," Tartarus states, "what do we get out of this proposal of yours?"

"You get to expand your influence onto my planet. You will gain territory and control. Our joined forces will squash their resistance. They don't have the strength of numbers to match our magic and armies."

Visions

"So, you are thinking of attacking my planet," Sarah pipes up. "What gives you the right to just attack my world?"

"Earth is in turmoil and needs to be resurrected," Mohryia says.

"And you believe this power-hungry warmonger?" Sarah says. "He has killed thousands with no regard to human life or any other life for that matter."

"The feisty one has a point, Mohryia," Daughtry says. "I say we do not attack her world without further proof that they are a threat to us."

"Well," Mohryia says, "they are planning a breach through the portal as we speak."

"Only because you have brought her here," Leylandria argues. "We could send her back and they would have no reason to enter our realm."

"My visions tell me that if I am not sent back to my world, yours will be in jeopardy."

There are a series of mumblings and discontent among the congregation of magical beings. "How so, young one?" Daughtry asks.

"The Greys and the Hybrids are getting ready to attack with their fleet on the other side of the portal."

More nervous chatter among them is heard.

"Tell us more," Leylandria says, leaning closer to Sarah.

"The Grey leader, Rodan, possesses the Crystal Codex and has the authority to use it."

"What?" Mohryia asks. "She's lying, the races have banned its use."

"Is this true, Sarah?" Leylandria asks.

"I don't know, but I do know what I saw. Rodan and his fleet have the Codex and are ready to use it."

"In your vision," Daughtry asks, "have they set it off in our world?"

"I couldn't tell."

"See, she lies!" Mohryia pounds his fist on the table.

"I'm not lying," Sarah counters. "I woke up before I could see more."

Just then Timmons enters from the hall in a panic and whispers in Mohryia's ear. "Very well," the evil wizard says, frowning. "Rodan and his fleet have breached the portal and should arrive within hours. We have no choice now. We must ready our troops for battle."

"Couldn't we just give them Sarah?" Leylandria poses.

"It's too late for that," Mohryia insists. "Rodan seeks revenge for the loss of lives in New Albion."

"But, we are not part of that!" Shardee complains. Many of the other attendees voice the same sentiment.

"Either way, if you do not fight you will die anyway. Rodan will not spare you."

"No!" Sarah shouts as she pushes herself from the table. "Just give me to them!"

"My fleet is already on their way to intercept him."

"No!" Sarah shouts again. "My brother and friend Ricky will be with him."

Mohryia rises and readies to leave. "Make up your own minds, but if you do not join me, you will probably be attacked anyway."

"I'm not waiting to find out," Daughtry says. He hops to his feet and exits with everyone else. With Mohryia and the other warriors gone, Sarah flops back down in her chair in despair. "What can I do?" she says out loud.

"You can come with me," Leylandria says as she walks back from the hall.

"But, what about my brother and Ricky?"

"My warriors will not be flying with Mohryia. I will take you to safety and contact Rodan myself."

"Oh, thank you." Sarah wipes stray tears away as she follows Leylandria. "I'm so afraid for my brother and Ricky. Can you save them?"

"I don't know, but if we do nothing we certainly can't. Don't give up yet." Leylandria's ship is small but fast. Not only that but other wizards are with her against Mohryia.

"Who else has joined us?" Sarah asks, watching them depart the castle grounds.

"Let's see. Shardee and Preshad's troops are with us. Mohryia, Tartarus, Daughtry, Belinda, Mazore and Dracous are against us. It is a pretty even fight except for the Crystal Codex, but you said this Rodan has use of it as well?"

"Yes, I saw that in my vision."

"Well, I hope you're right. We are catching up with the others. Are you a sentient as well?"

"I think so, but I'm not sure of my powers. I do know that in the last few years they have gotten sharper."

"How old are you?"

"Fourteen, almost fifteen."

"You have entered the change to womanhood then?"

Sarah blushes. "Yes, I guess so."

"Good, your powers will continue to increase as you mature. I want you to focus on your brother. Your connection with him is stronger than with the others. Try sending him a telepathic message explaining our situation."

"Okay, I'll try," Sarah says, then closes her eyes and envisions Billy's face.

"Don't force it. You will be more successful if you let it flow from your consciousness like energy."

Sarah starts to sense the ships in front of them—Mazore, Daughtry, Belinda.

"Oh," she suddenly says. "Belinda senses my force. She's trying to block me!"

"*Belinda Scandalum*!" Leylandria says, flashing her jeweled wand. Sarah watches the battle between the two witches as if it were playing out in front of her. Belinda, wand in hand sending purple energy forward, is stopped for a second and Sarah tries to send her message to Billy, but Belinda's eyes send energy beams at her as well, stopping her vision.

"*Sarah Scandalum!*" the blond witch yells. Sarah's thoughts are frozen and she can't see beyond Belinda's ship.

"I can't get passed her!" Sarah shakes her head and tries to force it.

"*Frigidus Belinda!*" Leylandria hollers as she sends energy streams at Belinda's ship. "*Dimittam Sarah!*"

Sarah feels her consciousness spring forward and fly to Rodan's ship. She sighs in relief and focuses on finding her brother. *Billy, can you hear me?* No answer. *Billy? Ricky? Answer me. I'm okay. Please answer me!*

"He cannot hear you. He is under my control." Mohryia's voice bursts through hurting her mind. Sarah shakes her head trying to break free of the pain.

Why? Where are they?

"With me, my dear. Safe for now, unless Rodan uses his weapon, or Leylandria and her traitors fire on my ship."

No, please. I will tell her to stop.

'Good girl. I have to say goodbye for now."

No, wait! I want to talk to my brother!

"Not yet, dearie. Later." Mohryia's words trail off as he breaks contact.

"Leyandria!" Sarah yells as she regains full faculties. "Don't fire on Mohryia's ship. He has my brother and Ricky captive!"

"Very well then. Fire on the others but not Mohryia!" She commands and her soldiers send volleys of energy at the other ships. Now the two fleets of warships are in fiery combat over the bright sky of Zeldor.

"But, how will we save my brother and Ricky?" Sarah wails.

"Calm down, young one. We will take care of the other warriors first, then chase Mohryia. Right now, Rodan is keeping him busy. See on the screen." Sarah watches the video screen as Mohryia's ship and Rodan engage in battle.

"What if one of them uses the Crystal Codex?" she asks.

"I think they are too close together to guarantee success without harming themselves. Oh, look, Rodan is backing off."

"Thank goodness!"

"And look, Daughtry, Mazore and Belinda have broken formation. They are leaving the battle. We just have Tartarus and Dracous to fight before we engage Mohryia."

Leylandria, Shardee and Preshad all focus their energy on Dracous and Tartarus. They are outnumbered and soon break off to escape the conflict. As they join the battle against Mohryia, Sarah notices an energy beam encircling his ship.

"What is he doing?" she asks.

"I don't know, but we better maintain our distance to be on the safe side." Suddenly, Mohryia's face appears on the screen of the ship. "Well, Mohryia, your allies have fled. You are outnumbered."

"Yes, but I have the Codex aimed at your ships. Back off or die!"

"If you use it, Rodan will annihilate you. He has the Codex too."

"You had better convince him not to use it as it will kill Billy and Ricky too."

"There's got to be another way!" Sarah says, hands shaking.

"Of course, there is," Mohryia answers. "Use your powers, Sarah, to convince Rodan to leave me alone and I will send the two young wizards to you unharmed."

"I'll try."

"You have five minutes to succeed." Mohryia's face vanishes.

"Can you reach him?" Leylandria asks.

"I think so," Sarah says, closing her eyes, and focuses on Rodan's ship. *Rodan, this is Sarah. Can you hear me?* No response. Sarah concentrates harder and enters the ship seeing Rodan in front of the comm. *Rodan, this is Sarah. Please hear me.*

"Sarah, hurry, you only have two minutes left," Leylandria says. Her words are distant, a faint whisper.

In her mind, Sarah presses her energy forward. "Sarah? Is that you?" Bhinder sees her ghostly image.

Yes, tell Rodan. Mohryia has Billy and Ricky held captive on his ship and is threatening to use the Crystal Codex. If you use it too, all will die! You have to let him go, now! Please!"

"But, he will escape and be back to terrorize us again," Bhinder argues.

"Sarah! Thirty seconds!" Leylandria's words pierce through.

You can fight him after my brother and Ricky are safe! Please! There are mere seconds left!

"Rodan, Mohryia is threatening to harm Billy and Ricky. You must stop before it is too late," Bhinder says.

"Pilot, disengage now," Rodan yells and his ship disappears in a flash. Sarah barely gets back to Leylandria as Mohryia comes on the screen again.

"Well done, young sentient, I knew you would be useful."

"Send my brother and Ricky!" Sarah shrieks at him. "That was the deal."

"The energy bubble around his ship is dissipating," Leylandria says. At the same time two shapes appear as a blur and then solidify in front of Sarah's eyes.

"Billy! Ricky!" She dashes to them, hugging them both.

"What happened?" I say regaining consciousness.

"Oh, my aching head," Ricky says from under her embrace.

"You're safe!" Sarah says, tears flowing, hands trembling. "Mohryia let you go."

"Whoa!" Leylandria says. "His ship has vanished."

"Good riddance!" I say. "I hope we never see him again."

"Where are we, anyway?" Ricky asks.

"You are on Zeldor," Sarah says.

"Yes, welcome, young wizards. I think you'll like it here. I'll take you to my village."

"I'm glad you're okay, sis. We were worried about you."

"I'm glad you guys are alright too, and I'll even be happier if we can get back home."

"I can take you through the portal, but for now come, rest, have a meal and learn of our culture," Leylandria offers.

"Sounds good," Ricky says after a yawn. "I could use some shut eye." The three of us laugh in agreement as Leylandria directs her pilot to her village. When we arrive, we're surprised by the variety of animals living within the city; dog-like and cat-like creatures with wings, horse-like ones with horns and one that looks like the mythical griffin, complete with wide wings, powerful jaws, and clawed feet. Another like a unicorn with wings.

"Wow, this is like going to ancient Greece," I say.

"Yeah, I wondered if some of those beasts actually existed," Ricky says. "I mean, here they are in the flesh."

"These creatures were first created by the ancient mystics of my world thousands of years ago," Leylandria tells them. "We have had to protect some of them from wizards who would use them for evil purposes."

"Anybody come to mind?" I say.

"Is that why Mohryia has brought some of these creatures to Earth?" Ricky asks.

"Has he?" Leylandria asks.

"Yes," Sarah says. "We've seen dragons and flying raptors."

"Dragons, we have. Raptors? I don't know what they are."

"They were an ancient creature, smaller than dragons and they didn't fly, I don't think," I say.

"He probably created them magically using other bird creatures," Leylandria says. "The ancient wizards fused characteristics of several creatures to make new ones."

"Did the ancient sorcerers of your planet travel to Earth?" Sarah asks.

"Possibly, as they knew of the portals in the universe," Leylandria confirms.

"So, the portals are like wormholes that can carry you to various realms?" Ricky asks.

"Exactly, our magicians have been capable of using them for millennia. We know of several other realms. Some magical, some not. But right now, you must be hungry, let's eat and rest."

"I'm all for that," Ricky agrees. Sarah and I laugh as Leylandria leads us into her castle through a huge gate. The animals cackle and whistle, happy their master has returned.

"This way, young wizards."

We follow her past the winged creatures and a crowd of cheering villagers along the stone steps to a set of stairs that lead up to a massive stone structure complete with high turrets, colored flags with a griffin on them. Soldiers stand at the ready with medieval weapons like great spear launchers, and others obviously used to drop hot water or oil on intruders. Inside the great hall, the walls are adorned with pictures of bearded men and longhaired women dressed in medieval looking outfits. Each of them holds a staff with a crystal embedded in it, much like Celtic druids of old.

"That one with the cone-shaped hat looks like Merlin," Sarah says, pointing.

"That is Merlin. How do you know of him?" our host asks.

"If that is the same one, he definitely traveled to Earth. There is a whole legend about him and his magic in helping King Arthur become a great leader of his people," Sarah says. "Our teachers told us all about him."

"Yes, he would have known how to travel to other realms, so I'm not surprised at all. He was my ancestor and this was his castle ages ago."

"Really?" Ricky says. "Then you and I are somehow related because Merlin is said to have introduced himself to many maidens back on old Earth and one of them was my ancestor."

"Welcome then, very distant cousin," Leylandria says smiling.

"Small universe, I guess," I say

Azandra

After breakfast, we stand on the front steps of the castle watching the villagers carry on their daily routine chores. It's so peaceful here that I begin to wonder why evil wizards like Mohryia have to be a part of it all. Evil always seems to be there trying to challenge the good in people's lives. I guess it is the Ying and Yang of the universe; positive and negative of existence; black and white; dark and light. You can't have one without the other.

"Billy, I think it's time for us to get back to our world and see what's left of it," Sarah says.

"Well, that sounds positive," I say sarcastically.

"You have to admit, the future hasn't been very enlightening," Ricky says.

"True enough," I answer. "Leylandria, I love your world and its happy people, but it's time for us to get back and take care of Mohryia before he completely destroys ours."

"Yes, and I will go with you to help you in this," she says.

"Thank you, we really appreciate your support and hope it doesn't cause more grief for you or your world," I say.

"If I do nothing, I am not guaranteed that Mohryia won't come back to finish me off anyway. I'd rather face him away from my subjects, to keep them safe."

Once Leylandria's ship carries us through the portal we head for New Albion, or what is left of it. I'm afraid of what Mohryia may have done against Rodan. "Sarah, can you sense anyone in the city?" I ask as the dome comes into view.

"Give me a second," she says as she closes her eyes and focuses. Leylandria opens the hatch with no problem, and we descend to the landing deck. "I sense people in the council chambers. Azandra is there."

"Anyone else?" I ask. "Mohryia? Rodan?"

"No. Just her and some of her soldiers." As we dock I notice debris all over the place, smoking, twisted metal and fires all over.

"Mohryia was here though," Ricky says. "He left a path of destruction."

"Let's find out what happened," I say as we step onto the landing deck. We're greeted by one of Azandra's soldiers. "What happened here?"

"Mohryia and Rodan had a battle just outside the city, but it started when Mohryia attacked inside. His troops demolished most of the city before Rodan came with the fleet," the soldier answers.

"Where are Rodan and Mohryia now?" Ricky asks.

"After the battle, Mohryia and his ships disappeared and Rodan went after them."

"Where are they now?" Leylandria repeats Ricky's question.

"Rodan sent a message that Mohryia had slipped through another portal. Then we lost contact with him and his ships."

"Okay, thank you," I say. "Is Azandra alright?"

"Yes, but much of our forces are depleted. If Mohryia comes back, we won't have a chance."

"Keep guard and warn us if he does," I say.

"Yes, I will," he answers, holding his weapon close. We head into the wrecked building to see Azandra.

"Are you okay?" I ask as we enter the great room.

"Yes, just feeling defeated." She runs her fingers through her hair in frustration; her clothes torn and dirty, and scratches still bleeding from her arms. "Rodan has gone after Mohryia."

"Do you know where they are?" Ricky asks.

"No, but he probably escaped through a portal. At least that's what Rodan's last message said. I can't track them through it."

"Sarah, can you tell us where they are or at least where they were last, before they disappeared?" Leylandria asks.

"Maybe?"

"Maybe with our help we can find them together," a voice speaks up from the back of the room. Mahrunda, Bhinder's twin sister, steps forward. Sarah and the twin hold hands, close their eyes and focus.

"What about Rhunella?" I ask.

"No, I'm afraid she's dead." Azandra shakes her head. "So much loss of life and devastation."

"I am sorry that you have to suffer such evil," Leylandria says.

"Yes, until Mohryia is captured or killed there will be no peace."

"I think we have something," Mahrunda says after several minutes. We turn and focus on the sentient. "Mohryia has gone through the portal to the past."

"Yes," Sarah adds, "through the E&N portal."

"Interesting," I say, "That's the first portal Ricky and I traveled through by accident."

"Yeah," Ricky agrees, "but why is he going into the past?"

"And, where is he?" I say.

"He's in our time, I think," Sarah says.

"Azandra?" a voice interrupts our conversation over the comm. "Azandra, answer."

"It's Rodan," the Commander says. "Yes, I'm here, Regent. Where are you?"

"I'm on my way back. We lost Mohryia. He escaped through another portal I think, but I can't trace him."

"Yes, we know," Azandra answers. "The young wizards are here with Leylandria from Zeldar. They will go after him."

"Good, I think that magic is the only way to stop him."

"I will see you soon," Azandra responds then clicks the comm off.

"Leylandria, can you take us to the portal?" I ask.

"Of course, but where is this portal?"

"We know exactly where it is," Ricky says.

"Yes," I agree." Sarah, we're going home."

My sister smiles. "It's about time. I bet Mom is wondering what happened to us."

— CHAPTER TWENTY-SIX —

Purple Eyes, Again

Looking down on the cold, white ice age below from Leylandria's ship, I can't help wondering what the future will be like if we alter some of the outcomes of the past. *If we defeat Mohryia, and he dies, how will this affect New Albion and the Outlanders? Maybe there will be no resistance to the ordered society. Is this a good outcome or a bad one?* I'm uncomfortable with the thought that we may alter the destiny of mankind and send it on a negative path. The stakes are high.

"Ricky and Sarah, are you worried about how we may change the future by destroying Mohryia?" I ask.

"A little, yes. If we change the future, it may make it worse for humanity," Ricky replies.

"On the other hand," Sarah says, "we may, in fact, help mankind create a more peaceful future without him."

"What should we do?" I ask.

"I think we still need to pursue him," Ricky says. "He may alter it without us interfering, anyway."

"True. What do you think, Sarah?"

"I agree with Ricky. We have no way of knowing what he will do or already has done. We need to find him just in case there's a way to ensure a positive outcome."

"Very mature, young lady," Leylandria says, picking up on the tail end of our conversation. "Your involvement has already impacted the outcome. If it wasn't meant to be it wouldn't have happened. You must complete your task, as it was intended."

"You make it sound like the universe has dictated our involvement whether we like it or not," I question.

"In a way, that is true. Every action in the universe has a consequence and once choices are made they cannot be reversed. The path is made, and it must be followed," Leylandria says.

"Spoken like a true wizard," Ricky says.

"Witch, my dear," she corrects him. "We have arrived at the portal. Let's go and I will help you meet your destiny."

With her prophetic words, we landed and set off on foot to the portal. Although we stand on snow mixed with ice, we can hear the rushing river below. "Sarah, be ready to lock onto Mohryia's coordinates as soon as we go through," I say.

"Already focused, big brother."

"Allow me," Leylandria says as she raises her wand, blue energy sparkling. "Hold hands and we will be there momentarily." We do as ordered and then she speaks the words that make it so. "*Uago nos praetariti!*"

A whirlpool of energy envelopes us and we fly through the portal in rainbow colors, the sides of the tunnel a blur. After a few anxious moments, we land on terra firma again surrounded by blue static mist and right on top of the Kinsol Trestle. Unfortunately, I hear a train whistle, indicating it's coming down the track from the north.

"Quick! Off the tracks!" I yell as we race across the trestle. We barely make it off the tracks as the slowing train passes us at the Kinsol stop.

"What were you doing on the bridge?" a woman asks us, concern lining her face.

"There's so much fog and mist, we didn't realize the train was coming," Sarah answers for us.

I wink at her and Ricky nods in agreement. "Well, you could have been killed!" the lady shrieks. "Your mother should be more aware of what you're up to." She stares at Leylandria.

"Yes, children, hurry up or we'll miss the train," Leylandria chimes in, winking at us.

"Hippy, dippy woman," the lady scolds as we rush past her.

"Right, Mom, we're coming," I say, almost choking from holding back my laughter.

Sarah giggles and Ricky shakes his head as we follow Mom to the train station. "Three tickets please," Ricky announces, fishing his wallet from his pocket.

With our tickets, we moved onto the platform where we give them to the conductor. The whistle blows and he yells "All aboard!" behind us.

"Sarah, can you sense Mohryia?" I ask when we're seated.

"Not yet." She closes her eyes, fists clenched.

"Remember," Leylandria says, "relax and let it flow."

Sarah takes a deep breath and settles into the seat. Ricky and I wait.

"Ricky, why don't we take a look around the train. I have a feeling that we're not the only long-distance travelers on it."

"Yeah, right," he agrees, and we head toward the other cars. Everybody appears to be tourists in the first car, so we continue to the next.

"Look at the lady sitting in the front seat," I say.

"Oh," Ricky whispers. "Purple eyes." As we look at her she blinks her eyes and smiles.

"Don't pay her too much attention or she'll be suspicious," I say as we pause in front of her for a second.

"Good morning, boys. It's a lovely, old train, isn't it?" she says, her eyes piercing into mine.

"Ah, yes, I like the way they've fixed it up. It's so authentic," I respond.

"Is this your first time on it?" she asks.

"No, we're doing a research project on it for our history class," Ricky says.

"Oh, well I won't keep you from your task then. Enjoy the ride," she says, flashing her purple eyes at us.

"Yeah, let's go, Ricky. We've got the other cars to check out yet."

When we're in the next car I turn to him. "What do you think?"

"I don't think she's just a tourist, and those purple eyes tell me she's probably from the future."

"Yeah, I just wonder whose side she's on. We have no way of knowing."

"We should mention it to Leylandria. She might have some ideas on how to find out."

"Good idea, mate," I say. "Let's go back and ask her." We opened the door and stepped back into the car where the lady was sitting, but she's not there.

"Oh, oh," Ricky says. "If she's with Mohryia, she's probably onto us already."

"We'd better check on Sarah and Leylandria." We hurry back to our seats, but they're not there.

"Let's give them a minute. They may have just gone to the washroom. You know girls, they like to go together," Ricky says.
I laugh. "Yeah, they do everything in pairs." We sat down and waited for them to return, but after ten minutes I begin to worry.

"It's been a while," Ricky says.

"Yup, maybe we need to check."

On our way to the washroom, purple eyes greet us.

"Hello again, boys. Something wrong?" She raises her eyebrows at us and a cold chill runs up my spine. "*Duratus!*" she shouts, her arm waving a wand at us. Instantly, Ricky and I feel our bodies start to stiffen.

Yanking my wand from my pocket before we freeze completely, I yell, "*Interficiam incantores!*"

"*Veni mecum!*" She hits us with a powerful spell. I can't counteract it quickly enough and we're swept into a whirlpool of her creation. "*Duratus!*"

"*Interficiam incant...*" I try to stop it, but the spell carries us along with our captor to somewhere else...

— CHAPTER TWENTY-SEVEN —

Mirror, Mirror...

"Where are we?" Sarah asks as she and Ley landria touchdown on a grassy field.

"I'm sorry, dear, but I didn't have too much choice with that witch ready to blow us up on the train."

"You could have warned me!"

"Actually, no, there wasn't time. Anyway, we're okay. I brought us to a place my great, great ancestor told me about on your planet. We are near Eilean Donan Castle in Scotland. Look at it. Is it not the most beautiful castle you've ever scene?"

"Ye..yes." Sarah takes in the tall, majestic walls and turrets as it sits overlooking the Isle of Skye. "We can walk to it on this bridge, but why did you bring us way over here?"

"It was the first place that entered my mind. I don't know a lot about your world, but I do know a little about the places Merlin knew of, as I've read his diaries at home on Zeldor. We should be safe here. I doubt the witch that attacked us will know of it."

"Okay, I get it, but what about Billy and Ricky? They'll worry about us." Halfway across the stone bridge she stops and breaths the fresh air of the sea, and watches the tide roll in and out as it slaps against the rock walls. "This feels like we dropped into a fairytale."

"A story about fairies, you mean? I'm familiar with such wee creatures in my world, but I don't remember Merlin writing about them in yours."

"Oh, there's lots of fairy stories here and in Ireland as well," Sarah says as she continues walking over the bridge all the way to the front gate of the castle. "There's a sign here," she says, stopping in front of it. "Tours daily: 10:00—17:00. I wonder what time it is now?"

"You're just in time, Lass, the tour starts in ten minutes," a man answers from inside the gates.

"We're not really—"

"What a great idea," Leylandria cuts her off. "Can we join the tour?"

"Of course, Madam. Come right in and look around at the souvenirs while you wait," the man with a kilt, tunic, and red-bearded face says in a heavy Scottish accent. They walk around and examine miniature castles, Scottish flags, full kilts and other outfits of the period—calendars with pictures of the castle and surrounding lands, small bagpipers, various Scottish whisky bottles, cheese biscuits and other foods on display. A man is sitting by an easel, a palette in his left hand, adding dabs of paint to a picture of the castle he is painting.

"Very lifelike," a woman is saying to him.

"Thank you," he replies with a broad smile.

"Why are we here when we should be searching for Mohryia?" Sarah whispers as the tour guide invites everyone to start the tour.

"Be patient. There's a reason that will become clear shortly," the off-world witch replies.

Sarah clears her throat in frustration but follows her along the corridor on the first floor, at the back of the group. As they go up the stairs to the second floor she begins to pick up on a spiritual connection.

"I'm sensing someone," Sarah says.

"Yes, follow it," Leylandria says, stopping to allow Sarah to take the lead. She stares toward a bedroom at the end of the long hallway. The rest of the tour moved on to another part of the castle leaving the two free to inspect the old oaken door, barring their passage. Sarah tries the latch, but it's locked. "Allow me," Leylandria touches her wand to the latch. "*Apertus*," she whispers. The heavy door unlatches and creaks as it opens. A gust of musty air greets them.

"I don't think it's been opened for a long time," Sarah says, her heart beginning to pound. Inside they see an old bed covered by a canopy. A huge mirror standing to the right of the bed catches Sarah's interest. She moves to it and pulls a white sheet off it. Dust flies and the mirror reflects the sunlight from the cobwebbed window into her eyes. "Agh!" Sarah covers her eyes with her hand. "Something about this old mirror. It's piercing into my mind. Ow, it hurts!"

"Step away," Leylandria says. "*Revelet Deus absconsa tua!*" Blue sparks from her wand enter the mirror. At first, nothing happens, then the mirror reveals a face of a woman with long reddish hair, green glowing eyes and a pale face.

"I am Corrand, Guardian of this gateway. Who are you?" she questions in a harsh tone.

"I am Leylandria of Zeldor, descendant of Merlin."

"Merlin? I knew of a Merlin many ages ago. He sought me out. He was one of the greatest wizards in this realm. Why have you sought my services, witch of Zeldor?"

"We need your help in finding a wizard in this realm."

"And who would that be?"

"Mohryia."

"Oh, that name carries evil with it. He is a disruptor. I have seen his dark doings. Why do you search for him?" She wrinkles her face. "Are you in league with him?"

"No, we wish to stop him," Sarah says.

"And who might you be, young witch?"

"I'm Sarah, a seer and my brother and friend are wizards who may be in danger. Please help us!"

"What are the other wizards' names?"

"Billy Maclean and Ricky Stevens."

"Let me see," Corrand says, "ah, yes, Mohryia...I see him in the New World, oh I mean Canada...ah, Victoria."

"That's my home," Sarah says. "We need to go back!"

"Wait, another witch is with him, her name is Nahdahlia. She is a powerful ally of Mohryia. He has recruited her to destroy the young wizards. They are captive in Lord Dunsmuir's castle, I mean Craigdarroch Castle as it is now called."

"Can we get there?" Sarah asks in desperation. "Yes, there is another mirror in that mansion which I can connect you to. A simple spell and you can be there in seconds."

"But, we must be careful," Leylandria says. "Without disguises we will be spotted by Mohryia or Nahdahlia right away. I will cloak us first."

"Make us tourists. They visit the building all of the time," Sarah says.

"Let me see," Leylandria says. "How about mother and daughter from..."

"Scotland," Sarah finished for her. "I'll use my grandmother's accent." She breaks into a heavy Scottish brogue. "Make the clothes modern though, or else we'll look out of place."

"*Mutate vestimenta*," Leylandria says, and her clothes match more closely to Sarah's.

"Keep mine modern but change them too. Remember, I was seen in these."

"Right," off-world witch agrees. "*Mutate vestimenta Sarrae.*"

"Alright," Corrand says, "are you ready?"

"Yes," Sarah answers, stepping up to the mirror. Leylandria takes her hand as the mirror wavers and the guardian disappears.

"*Aperire animo ibi*," the guardian's voice says. The mirror's surface wavers in and out, rippling like liquid. "Enter now," she directs them.

"Here we go," Sarah says and bravely steps through the mirror with Leylandria right behind her, their hands joined.

— CHAPTER TWENTY-EIGHT —

Craigdarroch

A cold wind batters Sarah's ears as they are pulled through the magic tunnel. A few moments later, a light at the end grows quickly, larger and larger until they stop right in front of it. She can actually see into the room on the other side like looking through a window. At one point a little girl looks right at the mirror admiring her reflection. "Mommy, look, I'm a princess," she says as she pirouettes.

"What if they see us? What can we do?" Sarah asks.

"We wait," Leylandria answers. "Don't worry, they cannot see us."

They watch as the troop of tourists inspects the contents of the room. Sarah spies an old canopy bed much like the one in the Scottish castle they just departed from. A Victorian style dress hangs over a chair in front of a dresser, where fancy marble hairbrushes sit along with old metal containers for powders and creams, various sized combs, scissors and hairpins.

After several minutes the tourists moved on. "I think we can enter now," Leylandria says. She touches the mirror with her wand. "*Aperire animo ibi.*" The mirror's surface ripples again allowing them to pass through.

"I'm glad we're out of there," Sarah says. "I was getting claustrophobic."

Leylandria snickers. "Can you sense the wizards?"

"Yes, as soon as we entered this side, I felt my brother's presence."

"Where are they?"

"In a hidden tunnel below the castle. Follow me." The two exit the Victorian bedroom and descend two sets of stairs into a basement area. People are eating and drinking along several tables set up for the tour. She studies the large space carefully until she spies a doorway chained off. "Behind that door is the tunnel we need to go down."

"We'll have to wait until lunch is over," Leylandria says. "Are Mohryia and Nahdahlia with the boys?"

"No, they're in another passageway further down the tunnel. We might be able to free the boys without them knowing."

"Hmm." Leylandria pauses for a moment. "Come into the washroom with me for a second." She enters a washroom and Sarah follows obediently. "Make sure we're alone." Sarah checks the stalls until she's certain nobody is in them.

"All clear," she says.

"I'm going to make us invisible, okay?"

"Yup."

"*Et invisibilia nobus*," Leylandria says, waving her wand. Sarah doesn't feel any different, but when a lady steps in to use the washroom, she nearly runs into Sarah. Quickly dodging her, they both exit.

At the far side of the luncheon, they stop in front of the chained exit to the tunnel. They both carefully step over the chain and Sarah reaches for the doorknob, but of course, it's locked.

"*Apertus*," the witch whispers as she taps the doorknob with her wand and the lock clicks audibly.

They step into the musty tunnel. "Focus on the wizards."

"Billy and Ricky are below," Sarah says as they descend an old stone winding staircase.

"Where are Mohryia and Nahdahlia?"

"They're still down the tunnel, but we'd better hurry just in case they come our way." At the end of the lower portion, they come across a fork in the tunnel.

"Which way do we go?" Leylandria asks.

"Take the right passage." At the next turn, there's a doorway on the left side. "In there," Sarah says, "but Mohryia and the witch have sensed us. Hurry, they're coming."

"*Apertus*," Leylandria says, turning the knob at the same time. Inside, Billy and Ricky are startled by their appearance.

"Leylandria! Sarah! How did you find us?" Billy shouts.

"Quick, before Mohryia and that other witch catch up to us," Ricky says.

"*Dimiterre eos!*" the off-world witch says, tapping the chains holding the boys with her wand, freeing them.

"Hurry, they're coming." Sarah urges them all to flee immediately. The boys shake the cramps from their arms and legs then dash behind the two rescuers. As they ascend the stone stairs a flash of red strikes the wall behind them.

"*Duratus!*" Billy shouts, sending a blast of blue energy backwards with his wand.

"Go ahead," Leylandria yells, stopping behind them. "I will deal with the witch."

"*Duratus!*" Nahdahlia shouts and sends a red bolt at them.

"*Eaque declinet in!*" Leylandria counters and deflects the spell, which bounces harmlessly against the wall.

"*Eam ad mortem!*" Nahdahlia sends a death dart.

"*Declinet!*" Leylandria deflects the spell again. "*Arma eius! Arma eius!*" Before the witch can react, her wand is pulled from her hand and off-world witch grabs it.

"*Valeo!*" Nahdahlia turns away and disappears.

"*Ne illi magia!*" a voice shouts from the darkness, and a powerful bolt of energy flashes forward.

"*Declinet!*" Leylandria counters unsuccessfully, struck by the red flash. "Ah!" she screams as the energy paralyzes her. She falters and falls to her knees, dropping her wand.

By this time, the boys and Sarah have reached the door to the eating area. As they appear in the room people notice and turn their way but say nothing. "Where to now?" Ricky asks.

"Follow me," Sarah answers, immediately dashing for the stairs. When she reaches the bedroom with the mirror, a tour is going through so they must wait.

"What's in here?" Billy asks.

"A magic mirror," she answers, looking nervously for any sign of Mohryia. After a few minutes, the tourists flied out of the room. "Over here." Sarah leads us to the mirror.

"How do we use it?" Ricky asks.

"A special spell," she says. "I think I remember it. *Aperire animo ibi*?"

"Sounds right but are you sure that's it?" I ask.

"I think so," Sarah answers.

"We'd better hurry," Ricky says, "Mohryia's here and he's got his wand raised."

"*Aperire animo ibi!*" I say, tapping the mirror which starts to ripple.

"*Duratis!*" Mohryia yells just as we enter the mirror. Sarah and Ricky make it through, but I'm struck by the spell and freeze in the room.

"Well, I have two of you now," Mohryia says walking up to me. He touches his arm with his wand and says. "*Veni mecum.*" We disappear in a swirl of light.

— CHAPTER TWENTY-NINE —

Which Future?

I wake up with a start, bump into someone beside me and realize that it's Leylandria. I shiver and try to flex my muscles, but I'm bound by a chain attached to the wall behind us. We sit on a cold stone floor, in a jail of sorts facing bars through which I can make out two Outlander guards sitting on chairs talking, beside a fire.

"Leylandria, wake up." I shake her lightly.

She startles, looking around. "Where are we?" "I don't know. Some kind of dungeon. I think we're in the future again because there's an Outlander guard watching us."

"We must be in one of Mohryia's strongholds. Where are Sarah and Ricky?"

"They escaped through the mirror, but Mohryia froze me before I could enter."

"I'll see if I can enchant the guards," Leylandria says, focusing her vision on the guard facing us.

"You have not won yet," the guard is saying. "I get to exchange three cards. Do you want to bet on them?"

"Why not," his companion says. "I know my hand is better than yours even without your drawing. I raise you 50 quatres, Bozar." He laughs and slaps the table.

"Fifty quatres it is," Bozar says. "I'm feeling lucky tonight." He places three cards from his hand face down and retrieves three more from the deck, screws up his face and falls silent.

"Raise you another 50," his friend says, laughing again.

He's cheating you. Leylandria imposes her thoughts on Bozar's mind. The guard shakes his head as though trying to detach a mosquito. *He took his card from the bottom of the deck.*

"What!" Bozar says, shaking more violently.

Ask him.

"Well, are you going to match me?" the other guard insists.

"Why should I when you are a cheater?"

"What! You calling me a cheat?"

"You took your last card from the bottom!" Bozar accuses.

"I did not!" the guard with his back to them yells, throwing his cards on the table and drawing his knife.

"I know you did, Mordel! You always cheat!" Bozar shouts and jumps up, his knife drawn.

They stand leaning over the table poised to fight.

He's always hated you—wanted to kill you.

"You've always hated me!"

"What? Are you crazy? I'm your friend."

He's jealous of you because Mohryia trusts you more.

"You pretend to be my friend, but you want to take my place, beside Mohryia." He lunges at Mordel who backs away, and then jumps over the table grabbing Bozar's fur coat and stabbing at him.

"Ah!" Bozar yells, blood spurting out of his chest, and slashes at his friend catching him in the neck. Mordel screams and the two roll onto the floor slashing and punching. After a few minutes of this they both fall silent.

"Good work. They've eliminated each other," Billy says. "But how can we reach the keys?"

"I want you to focus with me and we'll extract them from his belt," Leylandria says.

We both concentrate and zero in on the keys, which won't detach from Bozar's belt.

"*Claves, venerunt ad me,*" she says. The keys wiggle a bit towards us but won't detach. "Try with me." "*Claves, venerunt ad me,*" we say together. The keys stretch and stretch until suddenly, they pop free and fly towards my fingers. I catch them and give them to Leylandria who undoes my chains. I rub my sore wrists and unlock my cellmate. We exit the cell.

"The key now is to locate my wand and not get caught. With it I can take us anywhere."

"It will be with mine, close to Mohryia or Nahdahlia for sure. We'll have to be smart if we want to fool them."

"Let's make ourselves invisible to start with. *Et invisibilia nobis*," Leylandria says and we both blend in with the room. "Now, let's find a place to hide nearby without tipping them off."

"Follow me," I say, heading up the stone steps. At the top I turn to the left towards the great hall. "Looks deserted. Let's wait here and see where Mohryia and Nahdahlia go."

We don't have long to wait as we watch Mohryia, Nahdahlia, Azandra and Rhunella enter the hall.

"Yes, of course, Rhunella," Mohryia is saying as he enters first. "We will honor Rodan's request for supplies to the new Lunar Colony as long as he provides more Element 117."

"He assures me, President, that the precious element will be sent right away," she answers. Several councilors follow them into the room and take seats around the huge table.

"It looks like Mohryia has changed the future," I say to Leylandria.

"We must return to the past to right it."

"But, where are Sarah and Ricky?" I whisper.

"Probably in the past, safe, I hope. I sense my wand. Nahdahlia has them both with her."

"We'll have to somehow separate her from the group. I have an idea. Let's go to the Central Control Room," I say, leading us out of the hall. With the wizards busy it's fairly easy to make our way down the halls. We encounter a few Outlander soldiers who are oblivious to our presence. Mohryia has certainly adjusted the future to favor his interests. I wonder if it's even possible to change it. Are we in a parallel universe or is this truly our own future, altered?

"Well at least the command center looks the same," I say as we enter. All of the screens show various images of New Albion including the Great Hall. "Use your mind tricks to have the comm operator call for Nahdahlia."

Leylandria nods and focuses on the intended target. *Nahdahlia is requested in the control center right away.* Nothing appears to happen except the operator looks around confused.

Nahdahlia's presence is requested in the control center immediately. The operator fidgets with the panel buttons, shakes his head, pauses, and looks around again. *Call Nahdahlia to come to the control center right now!* He reaches for the comm button and presses it. "Excuse me, councilors, but Nahdahlia's presence is requested in the control room immediately."

We watch the screen as Nahdahlia looks up, turns to Mohryia who waves her on, rises and heads out of the room.

"Let's confront her in the hallway where there are less people around.".

I agree and we step into the hall. Nahdahlia has just turned the corner. "*Duratus!*" I shout and she freezes in mid-step. "Get the wands." I say to Leylandria. She darts over and retrieves them.

"Let's go." She tosses my wand to me. "What time should we go to?"

"Well, if Ricky and Sarah went through the mirror just before I was caught by Mohryia, where would they have gone?"

"Yes, of course, to Eilean Dolan castle in Scotland. If I focus on the room with the mirror, I can get us there before they show up."

"What does that do to the future?"

"Let's see, we would not be captured by Mohryia so none of this future would look the same I don't think, at least not with us in it, but we still have to stop him."

"Okay, let's go."

"Hold my hand," Leylandria says, then poises her wand. "*Nos ad praeteritum Eilean Dolan.*" Instantly, we swirl into the time tunnel and stop abruptly inside the room of the old castle. Fortunately, no tour is present.

"That was lucky," I say. "I hope your timing is right."

"Look, the mirror is wavering." Leylandria points. Ricky and Sarah climb out of the looking glass, none the worse for wear.

"Boy, are we glad to see you guys," Ricky says. "We thought we'd lost you back there."

"Actually, you did, but we've fixed what happened," I say.

"What?" Sarah says, "how?"

"Don't worry about that now. What we have to do is stop Mohryia."

"And how do we do that?" Sarah asks.

"We have to go back and deal with him and Nahdahlia," Leylandria says. "The only problem is that with the changes we've already caused, we may have inadvertently changed the past too."

"What does that mean?" Ricky asks.

"We should be ready for anything. Wands out. The most important thing is to stop Mohryia from changing the past," I say.

"Ready then?" Leylandria says. "I suggest that Sarah and I go first to locate them."

"That makes sense," Ricky says. "How long should we wait?"

"Only moments, but it will be enough to catch him off guard, I hope," Leylandria says. "We'll use the mirror so that we end up at the same place and time. Ready, Sarah?"

"Ready as I'll ever be," she says, holding the off- world witch's hand.

"*Aperire animo ibi!*" Leylandria says and the mirror ripples. She and Sarah step through.

"Give them a few moments," I say to Ricky. We both counted out loud to ten.

"Let's go," Ricky says. "Aperire animo ibi." We step through. Leylandria and Sarah are already in the room waiting for us. Nobody else is with them.

"Hi, boys. We're in luck. We've located Mohryia and Nahdahlia," Sarah says.

"Where are they?" I ask.

"Actually, they're leaving the castle grounds," Leylandria says. "We'll have to hurry to intercept them before they transport."

"Yes, there's a portal just outside the back of the castle grounds, down a hill," Sarah says.

"Let's get going then." Leylandria leads us down the stairs, with her wand in hand. At the back door of the main room, we see the two wizards rushing down the steps. Nahdahlia turns and sends a blast of red fire at the doors. They blow open, swinging off their hinges, glass flying everywhere, just missing my face as I reach the doorway.

"*Et volavit ad me!*" Leylandria shouts and flies right through the door after them. Another red blast slashes the air like a thunderclap and the off-world witch is forced to dip and dive.

"*Duratis!*" she yells as blue streaks track Nahdahlia, who screams and falls beside a tall oak.

"*Cadent!*" Mohryia shouts, firing a bolt of red energy.

Leylandria dodges the spell and fires back. "*Duratis!*" She alights on the ground and takes cover behind the tree where Nahdahlia is lying.

"*Duratis!*" I shout, sending spells Mohryia's way from the porch. Ricky has rushed down the steps and is trying to catch up with Leylandria.

As he pauses on the lawn, Mohryia yells, "*Cadent!*"

The spell hits the tree, catching Ricky on the shoulder. He shouts and falls in front of Nahdahlia. "Ricky!" I yell, catching up with him and falling to his side.

"He's okay, just stunned," Leylandria reassures me. "Come, we have to stop Mohryia before he escapes through the portal." Sarah stops to take care of Ricky and the off-world witch and I pursue the evil sorcerer.

In front of us, just before the stone wall surrounding the castle, we see him casting a spell. "*Aperiesque ostium!*" We watch as a circle of wind and sparks appear, spiraling with a force that pulls leaves and dirt towards us. He looks back, smiles and waves as he jumps into the vortex.

"Quick, after him!" Leylandria says as we rush forward, the portal shrinking rapidly. We enter before it closes. The last thing I hear is Sarah shouting my name as I pierce the shivering veil and fly headlong into the tunnel.

— CHAPTER THIRTY —

Zeldor, Again

Leylandria and I roll out onto a meadow of green grass and flowers. "Welcome back to Zeldor," Leylandria says.

I stand and survey the surroundings. "But where is Mohryia?"

"He probably is back at his castle. This way." She steps towards the woods in front of us. "Let's hurry, it'll be dark soon." I look at the low golden rays of sunlight partially blocked by the tall trees. "Have your wand ready. There are dark creatures in the Gravesward forest. They do not take kindly to strangers and Dracous is not an ally of ours."

"Great." I glance around ready for anything as strange squawks and shrieks assault our ears. "What kind of creatures are in these woods?"

"Saber cats, werewolves, bears, deer, ravens, eagles; the usual, oh, and dragons, of course."

"Are there any weird or unnatural creatures?"

"You mean wizard designed? Very likely."

"Great," I say. "You're making me feel so much better."

"Sorry, but you wouldn't want me to lie to you, would you?"

"Of course not, I just was hoping that things would be a little easier to deal with."

"Really? Not when you're a wizard, young man."

"I guess I should be used to it by now. Whoa, what is that!" I say as a pair of bright red eyes slowly descends within a black-winged creature.

"Those are seekers. Dracous must have sent them our way." Several of them circle around us. "They can't harm us. They'll just tell the wizard where we are. Be ready, he may send soldiers to apprehend us." I pull my wand out just in case as we make our way through the darkening woods.

"*Illucio!*" Leylandria says and her wand lights up the night.

"*Illucio!*" I say and light the path in front of me as well.

We carry on for several minutes with the seekers following us left and right. "Stop," Leylandria suddenly says, her hand raised in warning. "Soldiers ahead of us. Follow me along this other path." She backs up and turns to the left where there is a less travelled path between the tall trees. I struggle through brambles and roots trying to follow her. We keep our light dim as we proceed, until we reach a rock overhang in our path.

"*Perimo!*" my companion says extinguishing her light.

"*Perimo!*" I say, my light goes out and we sit in the dark.

"Watch behind," she directs.

I look around just in time to see a horde of hooved creatures with horns on their heads running about ten yards away from us, their grunts and stomping clearly following them, lit torches carried in front. Luckily, they don't notice that we've taken another path and carry on away from us. We wait for them to leave before we continue.

"*Illucio,*" Leylandria says and the rock lights up. "There should be a cave not far from this outcropping." She steps around it to the right where a new path opens up. We climb over a little knoll into a short meadow until we reach more rocks rising up to the sky.

All of a sudden, a troupe of Dracous' warriors appears behind us. "Get them!" a large horned creature yells and bowmen and other soldiers fire weapons at us.

"*Protegat nos!*" I cry while surrounding us in a protective shield as arrows and energy beams deflect away from us.

"*Duratus!*" Leylandria shouts and freezes two of the warriors.

"*Duratus!*" I yell and two more stop in their tracks, but several others are catching up to us.

"Quick! There's the cave!" she shouts, and hits two more with her wand as we scramble through the entrance. "*Haec signa cave!*" she chants and the entrance closes just as energy beams follow us in. "*Protaget!*" The beams deflect on the walls and dissipate.

"What do we do now?" I ask.

"We go further into the cave. There's an exit a ways in."

"Why don't we just transport to the castle?"

"We can't from in here. The walls have been enveloped in a spell which inhibits magic. I know because I've been here before. "*Illucio*," she says, lighting up our way. "We must get through it quickly before the troops catch up with us on the outside. We can't just appear at the castle anyway, Mohryia will be expecting us. We need to catch him by surprise."

"And how do we do that?" I ask as I race to keep up with her while navigating slippery rocks and loose boulders.

"Hurry, I'm thinking about it."

After several winding passages, narrow walkways around huge caverns and slogging through marshy, stinky layers of bat-like guano, we come to an opening which leads us back out into the darkness.

"Good, they haven't made it around the mountain yet. We'll put some distance between them and us. "*Nos extra castra in Mohryia!*" Leylandria says, grabbing my hand. In an instant, we're transported to the outside of Mohryia's castle walls, in the meadow. I roll with her in the grass as we land.

"You could have warned me," I object as I regain my feet.

"There wasn't time. I sensed Dracous' presence where we were. Even now he may have followed us," she says, flashing her wand in expectation around us, but nobody seems to have followed us. "Now, we need transportation. *Phenera, venit ad me! Protanus venit ad me!*" Two big dragons appear coming from the east in great haste. They swoop and dive as they approach, until alighting gently on the grass in front of us. "Good boys." Leylandria walks over to them, patting their heads as they bow to receive her gratitude. I cautiously do the same. The huge beasts smile at me.

"At your service," the bigger one with red scales says, then proceeds to pick his teeth with a sharp claw, ending up pulling a chunk of meat from between his huge canines, throwing it back towards the woods. "Excuse me," he says, "I had breakfast in my teeth." The other dragon giggles, his tuft of golden hair on the back of his head shaking. He licks his teeth with his tongue and swallows some left over meal as well.

"We need you to take us to Mohryia's castle, but we must be cautious as he will be expecting us. He wants nothing more than to kill us," my witch partner says.

"Oh my, why would he want to harm us?" the smaller blue beast asks.

"We are no longer allies," Leylandria answers.

"Oh, I see," the other dragon says.

"So," the witch continues, "we must be invisible. Come, Billy, mount your dragon. Protanus, lower for your new master." The blue dragon lowers his body to allow me to climb onto his back. There's a saddle on his back already with footrests. It'll make the ride more comfortable.

With both of us on board Leylandria swishes her wand and says, "*Et invisibilia nobus!*" The two growling chariots take off and we disappear as we ascend into the air. "Quiet, boys, not a sound!" After half an hour or so, I can see Mohryia's castle ahead. "Slow, boys, fly past so I can see if there are any detectors. Keep your distance from the gates." The dragons slow down and detour around the front gates, leaving a good hundred yards' distance as we pass. Nothing seems amiss. All is quiet. "It is strangely quiet," the witch says. "Fly over to that group of trees. We'll hide there until we can decide how to proceed." We land just past the trees, close enough to see the castle without being seen. As we stretch our legs and drink some water from a river nearby, I notice a group of riders approach us from the far hills to the west.

"Who are they?" I ask as Leylandria makes us visible again. "*Nos visibili!*" she says as the riders stop and wait a few yards away. Shardee and Preshad lead their troops. "Welcome, brothers, you are here to support us against Mohryia?"

"Of course, sister, and Mazore is on his way as well," Shardee says.

"Thank you for helping us rid this planet of the evil wizard," Leylandria says. "What of the others?"

"Dracous is still allied with Mohryia, but the others have decided not to fight either way," Preshad answers.

"How should we attack?" Shardee asks.

"We need to attack in various ways or we will face his evil, one on one, and Mohryia is quite powerful, especially with the Crystal Codex," the witch says.

"Yes, well, at least one of us will need to meet him head on while the rest attack separately," Preshad suggests.

"That makes sense. I'll attack head on," Shardee says, "as I have the most troops."

"Alright, and I'll attack at the back to confuse and thin out his forces," Preshad says.

"Billy, you and I will attack from within," my witch companion says.

"Sounds, good."

"Shardee, you and Preshad attack the castle first to preoccupy him. Billy and I will enter the castle and weaken him inside."

"Okay, Leylandria," Shardee answers. "My forces, follow me to the front gates!" His troops, mostly on horseback, charge ahead with him, followed by a dozen dragons and other beast-soldiers with horns, armor and swords, on foot.

After they have advanced, Preshad addresses his men and beasts. "Soldiers, follow me around to the back of the castle!" His forces, including men on horseback, flying dragons and beast-soldiers on foot circle the castle.

"We'll give them a bit of time to engage Mohryia before we enter the castle," Leylandria says to me.

"Alright." I rest under a tree and think about Ricky and Sarah. *I hope they are safe in New Albion or wherever.*

After a brief rest, Leylandria alerts me by calling to the two dragons. "Protanus! Phenera! Prepare for us!" The dragons move away from the trees they have been munching on, growl, spread their wings, and lower themselves for us.

"Yes, master," Phenera says as Leylandria mounts him.

"Come, Billy, let's fight," Protanus says, bowing for me to mount him.

"*Fac nobis invisibilia!*" Leylandria says, and we disappear as our fiery steeds carry us towards the castle. I can clearly see the fierce battle at the front gates. Mohryia's soldiers are sending rocks out with catapults, striking Shardee's men while his dragons are firing flames at them from above, exchanging blows with the castle dragons over the embattlements. Buildings are on fire and crashing down, Shardee is bringing down the gates with spells.

"*Aras portarum!*" he yells, bolts of blue from his wand striking the walls and gates, wrenching them apart. Hordes of Mohryia's horned beasts rush out to the battle meeting Shardee's men. A blood bath ensues. From the back of the castle, we can see Pre- shad attack at the rear wall, tearing it to pieces with his magic. His troops charge the castle from the back, beasts, men and creatures all engaged.

As we approach the castle, I can see Mohryia, standing on the highest perch, his wand glowing with red energy, preparing to cast a deadly spell using the Crystal Codex beside him, throbbing in purple rings of energy.

"*Congelo!*" Leylandria shouts, sending a blue beam from her wand towards the evil wizard.

"*Deflecto!*" Mohryia sends the beam back toward us. I have to dodge quickly, pulling Protanus up, the bolt just missing.

"*Prohibe!*" I shout, and send a strong blue bolt of my own, but Mohryia sends it back again and we barely dodge it.

"We will have to face him together on his own ground to defeat him," my witch ally says. "Follow me." I do as she says as we fly away from Mohryia and circle the back of the castle. "Ah-ha!" she says. "Over there!" She points to a dark, empty balcony. "*Inferius me,*" she commands and Phenera obeys, setting his master on the deck below.

"*Inferius me,*" I say, and Protanus sets me down as well. "We may have a chance if we stay invisible."

"Yes, but we cannot coordinate our attack if we can't see each other."

"What do you suggest?"

"You stay invisible, and I will try to make him think that I alone am attacking."

"Okay."

"*Visibilium,*" she says, wand appearing before she does. She runs through the castle towards Mohryia and I follow her closely. She stops behind a wall that separates us from him. "Let me attack first and draw his fire."

We can feel the intensity of the Crystal Codex as it powers up. The purple bands of energy vibrate and send waves of color in every direction. The force field causes static electricity to jump in purple streaks between the pillars and along the wall, making my hair stand on end.

Leylandria jumps out and shouts, "*Impedir!*" A blue bolt catches Mohryia off guard as he hesitates, and the purple streaks cease, but the bands keep throbbing in waves, assaulting my ears.

"*Va embora!*" Mohryia fires a spell at Leylandria, who bounces backwards just past me and onto the stone stairs.

"*Congelar!*" I yell, sending a blue bolt at him.

"*Desviar!*" He sends the bolt back, but missing me.

"*Embora!*" I shout and catch him before he can counter. He goes flying over the wall.

"*Voar!*" he shouts while tumbling. A bolt of blue just misses him as he soars back up towards us. I see Leylandria, wand in hand, sending spells at him, but missing.

"*Cair!*" I yell and the blue bolt strikes him. He falls to the ground but rights himself almost immediately, only to be struck by a spell from Shardee. It freezes him momentarily and Shardee contains him with a series of spells.

"How do we stop the Crystal Codex?" I ask.

"I'm not certain. We'd better get away from it!" my witch companion suggests, and we call for our dragon steeds. They lower themselves to the stone walkway. As we fly away the purple bands throb louder and encircle the whole castle. Shardee and his troops, along with Preshad and his men, abandon their battle and retreat from the huge ball of violet surrounding everything, including them. As it grows, we fly as fast as we can to escape the destruction.

When we are past the surrounding trees a bright ball of bluish-red accompanied by an intense roar fills the air. I look back to see the whole castle devoured by the fiery cataclysm. A wrenching shock wave ripples through the air striking down the troops on the ground. Only Shardee has escaped from what we can see. He's flying away from the carnage on his dragon, towards us, and rides the subsequent waves out of harm's way.

"*Nos proteja!*" Leylandria says, wrapping all of us in a protective bubble. The shock waves continue over us and pass harmlessly, dissipating far beyond the city.

"Where is Mohryia?" I ask.

"I'm not sure, but I assume he was incinerated by the Codex eruption," Shardee says.

"He couldn't have survived that!" Leylandria says.

"Well, he certainly is not a threat anymore, even if he did survive it!" Shardee says.

"Where's Preshad?" I ask.

"Unfortunately, he did not escape the force of the Codex. He is gone as are all of his troops," Shardee asserts.

"Oh, that's terrible!" Leylandria says. "If it hadn't been for his counterstrike we would not have succeeded."

"Can we go back and check over the destruction?" I ask.

"Yes, it should be safe now," Shardee states.

As we survey the damage I notice that none of the soldiers or creatures are visible; all I can see are piles of ashes with heat rising from the plains and buildings.

"What happened to the people?" I ask.

"The Codex reduced everything to ashes, all that remains is the scrub grasses, dust and the castle," Leylandria says.

"No wonder that weapon was banned," I say. "The carnage is horrible!"

"The castle is all that remains," Shardee says, "no creatures, no animals of any kind."

"No weapon either," I say. "It appears it's thoroughly annihilated itself as well."

"Come away from this gravesite," Leylandria says, "this is all too unpleasant." We fly in the opposite direction of the blast until we reach the vortex. "Finally, you can go home without worry of being attacked by Mohryia."

"Indeed," Shardee says. "If you ever need us, don't hesitate to come back."

"Yes, Billy," Leylandria says. "And invite my cousin Ricky as well." We laugh as I wave my wand.

"*Entre no vortice!*" I say, sending the spell into the circle of energy which opens up like a cat's eye.

"Goodbye, fellow magicians." I look behind at them waving to me as Protanus and I spiral into the vortex.

CHAPTER THIRTY-ONE

The E&N Escape

Protanus and I arrived back, not far from New Albion. I approach the city slowly and can see someone coming out of the portal in a pod to meet me.

Billy, you're safe!. A thought enters my mind and I recognize it as Sarah's. *Ricky is with me and we're both alright.*

"Excellent, but why didn't you wait in the city to meet me?" *I just couldn't, Billy. We all want to know what happened. Azandra wants to see you too.*

By this time, the pod is directly in front of us and I can see all three of them through the window waving at me.

"I'm going to send Protanus, my dragon, back to Zeldor. Follow me to the portal." The pod follows me to the portal where I say farewell to Protanus. "Thank you for helping us in this fight."

"Always," Protanus responds, then enters the portal.

Back in the pod with Sarah, Ricky and Azandra, all of them hug me. Purple eyes gives me a kiss on the cheek and thanks me for saving her people.

"Any news on Mohryia at all?" she asks.

"I think he was destroyed by his own weapon, the Crystal Codex, back on Zeldor."

"Good," Azandra says. "Let's go back and report your good news to New Albion."

In the city, a crowd awaits us as we exit the pod. Cheers go up and banners wave. Regent Rodan and the other councilors step forward.

"Congratulations, young wizards. Without you, we would have never defeated Mohryia and Nahdahlia. Come join us in a meal and celebration," Rodan says.

At the table, there are numerous bowls of fruit and plates of vegetables to biscuits, breads, and chocolates. It feels good to sit down and enjoy a real meal for a change. We also share a moment of silence for Rhunella and all of the other warriors that have fallen in the battle with Mohryia.

After the feast, we are honored with medals of gold. They are embossed with a dragon, the symbol representing New Albion, and a picture showing the galactic alignment of the solar system.

"Thank you for the recognition. It's been a learning experience for us, and glad we were able to help," I say.

"Your courage and help are commendable," Azandra says. We are congratulated by all with handshakes and supportive words.

"Thank you again," Sarah says, "but we would like to go back to our own time now."

"Of course," Azandra says, "but we cannot use the time chamber as it was destroyed in the battle."

"That's okay," I say, "just take us to the E&N Portal."

"Absolutely," Azandra says, "I'll go with you and see you off safely."

We say our goodbyes and head to the pod deck. As we fly to the portal, it's hard to believe this adventure is finally at an end. I expect Mohryia or some other evil wizard to pop out of the clouds and attack us, but nothing happens.

"Can you feel the portal?" I ask Sarah when we're on the ground.

"Yes. It's just over there by that field. Follow me." She tromps ahead through the snow and stops in the middle of a snowbank. "Right here."

Ricky and I stop beside her, and we say good-bye to Azandra who hugs all three of us, and gives me a kiss.

"I will miss you, young wizards," she says, eyes filled with tears.

"If you need us again just shine your purple eyes and we'll know," Ricky says. Azandra nods as she steps back towards the pod.

"*Abra o portal!*" I say, my wand sends blue energy beams into the air until an opening of swirling air and matter appears. I take one last look back at Azandra and her beautiful eyes before we walk into the vortex and fly into a tunnel of light and energy, quickly stopping right beside the train as it travels on the tracks.

"Wow!" Sarah says, "I guess that's better than landing on the tracks."

"Yeah," Ricky says, "and lucky nobody is standing here."

"Couldn't have timed it much better," I say. "We're right at the Kinsol Trestle."

"Wanna go for a walk on the trestle?" Ricky teases Sarah.

"Yeah, right," she answers. "I just want to go home." She slumps down on a bench just as we hear the engineer call, "All Aboard!" Ricky and I join her, watching all the tourists come onto the rail car.

Ricky elbows me as a girl with purple eyes passes us. She smiles but keeps on walking. "I hope those are just colored contacts," he says.

"No kidding, eh. We've had enough excitement for a while," I say.

"That's for sure," Sarah says, sighs and closes her eyes as the train jolts forward heading down island to our home.

After a while, I snooze with the motion of the train and dream about our latest adventure.

"Don't forget to visit," Leylandria says as we walk on the outskirts of her castle. Protanus snorts and smiles. "You can ride me whenever you're here," he says. "I'd like that," I reply. Phenera smiles as well, accompanying us on our walk. "So, did you ever hear any sign of Mohryia?"

"Funny, you should ask. Shardee said that he noticed something strange in the Bogwart Forest," the witch answers.

"What did he see?"

"A dark creature flying above the trees that looked sort of like a misshapen wizard riding a dragon."

"And no wizard lives there?" I ask.

"No, just swamp creatures, blackbirds, vultures, and such. No wizard in his right mind would be caught in that stench. It reeks of the dead and dying."

"But, what if a wizard wanted to hide while he regained his strength?"

"I doubt it. Mohryia was annihilated with the rest of the warriors in the battle."

"Billy, Billy wake up!"

Jolted from my sleep, I find Sarah shaking me. "We're in Victoria. Time to go home."

"Right, right," I complain. "I'm coming, I'm coming. You don't have to shake me to death."

"Come on, sleepy head," Ricky teases as we grab our belongings and shuffle off the train. "Do you think we've gathered enough information for our report?"

"I'm sure we have loads of stuff and, if not, we can always come back and travel some more," I answer.

"No, I think we should stay home for a while," my sister says. "I've done enough traveling with enough excitement for a whole year." The three of us laugh as the girl with purple eyes smiles at us and walks by.

<u>Magic Spells</u>:

Abra a portal----------Open a portal
Aperiesque ostium------Open a circle
Aperire animo ibi------Make a flexible membrane
Apertus----------------Open the door
Aqua Regelo - ---------Water thaw
Aras partarum----------Separate it
Arma eius--------------Make the weapon miss
Belinda scandalum------Send Belinda away
Cadent-----------------Hit
Cair-------------------Knock down
Claves, venerunt ad me-Keys, come to me
Congelo -------------- Freeze
Congelar---------------Freeze him
Congelo est Draco------Freeze the dragon
Deceptus Raptor--------Enclose/enwrap the beast
Declinet---------------Protect
Declinet ignus---------Protect from fire
Deflecto---------------Send back
Desviar----------------Deliver
Dimittam Sarah---------Send Sarah
Dumiterre eos----------Stop them
Dolorem -------------- Pain
Draco, contra eos------Dragon, attack them
Draconi----------------Dragons
Duratis/Duratus--------Freeze
Duratis puella---------Freeze all
Eaque declinet in------Decrease and drop it
Eam ad mortem----------Kill them
Embora-----------------To throw back
Entre no vortice-------Send the spell into a vortex
Et ascendere me--------Raise them to me
Et ignis hostes earum, Draco---Dragon burn them alive
Et invisibilia nobus---Invisible to all

Et volavit ad me-------Send me through it
Fac mihi interitum-----Make me invisible
Fac mihi apparet-------Make me appear in front of
Fac nobis invisibilia--Make us all invisible
Frigidus Belinda-------Stop Belinda
Futura praeturitis as nos--Take us to the future
Ignis ---------------- Fire
Ignis desino-----------Put fire out
Illucio----------------Light our way
Impedir----------------To impede
Impetus----------------Breath deep
Inferius me------------Put me down
In frigore et arioles--Make them freeze
In frigore milites-----Freeze soldiers
In me transierunt------Hide me
Inrita magicae---------Stop magic
Interficiam incantores-Stop the spell
Mensamque--------------Manage the table items
Mittet in ea New Albion-Send to New Albion
Mohryia et abierunt----Move Mohryia
Mutate vestimenta------Change clothes
Ne Draconum------------Stop the dragon
Ne illi magia----------Stop your magic
Nos ad Kinsol----------Take us to Kinsol
Nos ad praeteritum Eilean Dolan--Take us to Eilean Dolan castle
Nos extra castra in Mohryia---Take us to Mohtyia's castle
Nos visibili-----------Make us visible
Panthera---------------Lion
Perdere----------------Strike down
Perimo-----------------Light out
Phenera, venit ad me---Phenera, come to me
Prohibe----------------Stop
Protanus, venit ad me--Protanus come to me
Protegit---------------Shield me
Protegit nos-----------Shield us

Protegit nos a draconibus--Shield us from dragons
R*egello*----------------Thaw
Regello eos------------Thaw them
Revelet Deus absconsa tua---Reveal the spirit of the mirror
Sicubi incantatores----Deflect the spell
Sarah scandelum--------Send Sarah away
Super nos--------------Spare us
Uago nos praetariti----Go through portal
Ubi es, Ricky----------Where are you, Ricky
Ut me Mohryia----------Make me Mohryia
Ut mihi apparet--------Appear in front of
Ut mihi interitum------Disappear in front of
Ut maneant nobiscum----They both will disappear
Va embora--------------Throw you back
Valeo------------------Be gone
Veni mecum-------------Go to my place
Visibilium-------------Turn invisible
Voar-------------------Come back
Volantus ad Remotus----Change course

About the Author

Raised in Victoria, BC, Canada, P.N. Holland (Neil) writes in memory of his wife, Kris. He has two children, five grandchildren and two dogs. Neil has taught for over 30 years in Public Schools in British Columbia and holds an M.Ed from the University of Victoria with a major in English. His writing is fast-paced, and his stories are page-turners. Neil also likes to visit schools where he shares his insights on reading and writing with students and teachers alike. Neil is currently working on another trilogy called **Mellissadorha (Vahldor** is Book One), a collection of short stories and a detective series.

The E&N Escape is the third book in **The Vancouver Island Mysteries Series**. It, and the other books in the series, **The Saxe Point Park Mystery** and **The Lost Boys of Lampson,** are all magical mysteries with settings close to home. He has written a Teacher's Study Guide for The Saxe Point Park Mystery, which is being used to teach the novel. He is proud of the fact that his book is helping kids improve their reading and writing skills. Neil's books are available in softcover and eBook versions at libraries, bookstores and online (i.e. Indigo/Chapters, Amazon, Barnes & Noble).
Contact   https://pnholland.com/   or   https://filidhbooks.com for direct purchase options.

Don't miss out!
Visit the website below, and you can sign up to receive emails whenever P.N. Holland publishes a new book.
There's no charge and no obligation.
https://books2read.com/r/B-A-JLFK-MAKEB

www.ingramcontent.com/pod-product-compliance
Lightning Source LLC
Chambersburg PA
CBHW070757280626
47162CB00016B/1323